CLIFF
HANGER

CLiFF HANGER

Pamela Carrington Reid

a heart-pounding adventure by

a novel

Covenant Communications, Inc.

Covenant.

Cover image by Mark Sorenson markearlsorenson@gmail.com

Cover design copyrighted 2007 by Covenant Communications, Inc.

Published by Covenant Communications, Inc.
American Fork, Utah

Printed in Canada
First Printing: May 2007

11 10 09 08 07   10 9 8 7 6 5 4 3 2 1

ISBN 978-1-59811-330-3

New Zealand

Great
Barrier Island

Hauraki
Gulf

Auckland

Location Map
New Zealand

North Island

Auckland

Wellington

Christchurch

South Island

Dunedin

ACKNOWLEDGMENTS

I extend a very special thank-you to those New Zealanders who are dedicated to the protection of our ocean environment.

* * *

New Zealand Ministry of Fisheries
Auckland Dolphin and Whale Safaris
Great Barrier Information Office
Sea Lab
Residents of Great Barrier Island

To Jordan, who made the
Coffin House Kids a reality,
and to Olivia, Harrison, and Delta

CHAPTER ONE

"They're not really coffins," Wiremu Pokere murmured to himself as he briefly closed his eyes and squeezed past the end of a long, polished wooden box. "They're just pieces of wood . . . put together in a certain shape. It doesn't matter that they'll hold . . . bodies . . . someday."

He opened his eyes again but deliberately kept them focused on the small doorway ahead of him. He refused to allow himself to look up at the tall wooden racks that towered above his head—racks that held more coffins. He tiptoed across the room and tried to pull the door open, but it stuck at the bottom. He tugged harder, and it finally opened with a loud squeak.

Wiremu took a deep breath before calling out quietly. "Toni? Toni . . . are you up there?" His voice echoed eerily up the narrow staircase as he leaned forward carefully, resting his hand against the bottom stair. A shaft of light filtered through a slight opening at the top of the stairs, illuminating a silvery lacework of cobwebs. He gulped, then cleared his throat. "Toni? Are you there?"

"Yeth." Toni Bradford's voice was so muffled he could barely hear it. "Huwwy upf."

Wiremu took another deep breath and began to make his way up the winding staircase. He used the rolled-up newspaper in his hand to clear away a low-hanging spiderweb, but it clung to the paper in thick, gray tendrils, obscuring the print. He stifled a gasp as a large spider with a bulbous, black body suddenly ran across the ceiling above his head and disappeared through a tiny crack between the boards.

"Gross!" he muttered as he pressed himself against the wall, his normally brown skin going a shade paler as the roots of his curly, black hair prickled. He shivered, then shook himself.

"Wiremu! Hurry up!"

He recognized his cousin Erana's voice and frowned. What was she doing here? He took another shaky breath and rapidly climbed the last few steps in a crablike scuttle and tumbled through the narrow doorway into the attic.

"At wast!" Toni Bradford raised one eyebrow as Wiremu stood up and brushed off his sleeve. "You're wate."

"I'm 'wate' for a 'weason'." Wiremu grinned, and the laughter lines around his eyes immediately deepened as he observed both girls and began to chuckle. "Now I think I should have stayed away. What do you girls think you're doing?"

"Twying a new wook." Toni muttered around several hairpins clamped firmly between her lips and concentrated on pulling Erana Burgess's thick, black hair into a tight coil. "We fought 'ou were wost."

"We finished our homework ages ago." Erana grimaced slightly as Toni pulled a few strands too tightly. "What took you so long?"

"I was waiting for the newspaper . . . like I was supposed to." Wiremu held up the paper and began to pull the thick, gray webs off with his thumb and finger, his face screwed up in distaste. "And then I had to fight my way through giant spiderwebs and around coffins. Why you girls want to have our group headquarters here in the coffin house is beyond me. And you can't have finished your homework because you still haven't got your current-event item."

"That's the only thing," Erana retorted primly, then flinched. "Ouch, Toni . . . I'm beginning to think I should do this myself."

Toni sat back on her heels and took the clump of hairpins out of her mouth. She pursed her lips together and folded her arms as she regarded Erana's hair. The coil was rather lop-sided, and several pins jutted out among tiny, curling tendrils.

"I think you're right." She nodded thoughtfully, her long, silky blonde hair falling over her shoulders. "I think I'll stick with being a marine biologist rather than a hairdresser."

"You think?" Wiremu chuckled again and dodged as she tried to thump him. "But your location could be a real winner . . . 'Coffin House Coiffeur.' That could be a definite drawing card. People will be *dying* to get here . . . especially for Halloween." He laughed at his own joke while the girls shared an understanding look. Wiremu would never be lonely. He could keep himself amused for hours. "We could even provide the spiders." He manufactured a dramatic shiver. "Man, I hate spiders."

Toni sat back against a large, blue corduroy cushion and waited. She loved listening to Wiremu laugh and chatter just as much as she enjoyed listening to him and Erana argue without arguing. She and the cousins had become firm friends since she and her father had moved to New Zealand from Australia just a few months earlier, and already they had had their share of exciting times together.

She smiled as she thought about it. She had dreaded coming back to New Zealand after her mother and father had divorced, but life back in Australia suddenly seemed very quiet compared to all the things that had happened to her in the last few months—chasing "ghosts" in the coffin house, being held captive in a coffin, finding a runaway kid, and fighting off vicious dogs.

"So what's in the news? Anything interesting happening?" Erana settled down on a bright red cushion—one of several cushions they had brought up to decorate their new headquarters in the attic of the coffin house. In fact, the old attic looked quite comfortable now that they had decorated it with the pieces of furniture they had begged from their families. A small, low table sat against one wall, covered with neat stacks of paper and pots of pencils and pens and surrounded by more cushions in bold, rainbow colors.

"News . . . I forgot!" Wiremu smacked his forehead dramatically, then waved the newspaper in his other hand. "Have I got news for you!"

"That's what we're hoping for." Erana rolled her eyes and held out her hand. "Just show us."

"I will." Wiremu sat down beside the table and carefully moved the paper and pens before unrolling the newspaper. "You're not going to believe this."

"Believe what?" Erana held out both hands expressively. "You're not telling us anything."

"Well . . ." Wiremu nodded his head knowingly. "You won't believe it even when I do tell you."

"Wiremu!" Even Toni started to feel frustrated as she leaned toward the table. "What *is* it?"

She didn't hear his answer, because just then a loud clattering noise erupted from the stairwell, and a huge dark mass suddenly filled the doorway and swarmed toward Toni, knocking her to the floor.

"Help!" A strangled yell preceded another shape that fell heavily onto the floor beside Erana, pushing her to the side. "I couldn't stop her . . . and my hand's stuck!"

"Taseu . . . what . . . ?" Toni tried to sit up, but she was pinned against the wall. "Rima! Rima . . . Stop it!" With a laugh stuck in her throat, Toni put up her hands to stop the enthusiastic licking that threatened to remove her eyebrow.

"Rima! I love you too . . . but . . . stop!" She gently pushed the huge dog away and wrapped her arm around its neck. Rima sat down panting loudly, her wide mouth stretched into its perpetual grin.

"She was fine until we turned back to the coffin house." Taseu Ta'ala shook his head, beads of perspiration glistening on his forehead. "All I said was 'Let's go back and see Toni.' And she took off!

My hand got stuck in the leash." His eyes grew wide as he pulled the offending leash off his hand and rubbed his wrist. "I felt a bit like one of those windsurfer guys—like I was going to lift clear off the ground if she went any faster."

Toni instantly smiled at the vision of her chubby friend lifting off the ground, but it was Wiremu who snorted loudly.

"It would take a lot more than Rima to get you lifting off the ground." He chuckled and punched his friend's shoulder kindly. "Maybe a few more laps around the neighborhood like Miss Jenson says."

Taseu chuckled happily and made some running movements with his arms in slow motion. He was wearing a bright red shirt with large, yellow and pink hibiscus flowers printed all over it and bright yellow baggy beach shorts, which he changed into as soon as school finished each day. He was as predictable as Wiremu, who always wore the too-large nylon mesh basketball shorts and a black or white singlet. Today he was wearing black.

Toni grinned as she glanced around at the group. They all had such different personalities, and it showed in what they wore. Erana always preferred to stay in her school uniform, which consisted of a white polo shirt and dark green plaid skirt, and she always looked tidy with her thick hair neatly kept in one of a hundred different styles she experimented with. Toni sighed as she ran her hand through her long blonde hair and looked down at the basketball shorts she wore with her school polo shirt. Sometimes she wished she felt more feminine like Erana, but it usually only lasted until Wiremu wanted to play basketball or any other type of sport, or until she took Rima for a long walk or played with her.

As if hearing Toni's thoughts about her, Rima sighed deeply and leaned against Toni, almost pushing her off the cushion. Although Toni had been terrified of Rima on their first encounter, the two had become inseparable since Jack, Rima's owner, had gone to boarding school and left his dog in Toni's care.

"But Rima will be happy to be your personal trainer." Toni directed this remark at Taseu, then laughed as she cuddled the big dog around the neck and received an exuberant lick on her cheek in return.

"Excuse me. Speaking of Miss Jenson—" Erana tapped a finger on the newspaper. "She said we've got to have a news report ready by tomorrow, not next month."

"News, news, news." Wiremu held up his hand then pointed at the paper. "You guys keep interrupting me. How about this for news?"

They all leaned forward to look at the heading on the front page where his finger was pointing.

"Body discovered." Erana read out loud then wrinkled her nose. "Yuck!"

"Attached to buoy." Taseu finished reading the heading, then leaned closer to look at the small print. "A man's body was found by a local fisherman in the Hauraki Gulf yesterday afternoon. It was attached to lines from a buoy marking crayfishing pots and appears to have been in the water for several days."

"Eew!" Toni shivered. "Several days."

"Keep reading." Wiremu folded his arms. "It gets better."

"Better?" Erana frowned at her cousin. "The man died."

"Yes, but how did he die—and where?"

"It says that police suspect poaching of fish and suspicious circumstances." Taseu quickly ran his finger along the lines of print. "And . . . here it is—near Great Barrier Island."

"Poaching . . . suspicious?" Toni looked puzzled. "Does that mean the police think someone—"

"Killed him? Yes!" Wiremu nodded emphatically. "But did you get where he was found?"

"Near Great Barrier . . . Oh, my goodness!" Erana's eyes grew wide.

"Exactly! Great Barrier Island." Wiremu sat back and glanced around at them all, his expression actually serious for once. "And we're all planning to go there next week to help Uncle Ammon with his crayfishing!"

For several long moments the only sound was Rima's heavy panting, then even she seemed to sense their mood, and she sank down onto the ground with a low whine, her head resting on her paws. Toni instinctively reached out and stroked the dog's head.

"Do you think . . ." She hesitated and frowned. "Well, do you think maybe we shouldn't go to the island? I mean if there's been a murder . . . it could be a bit dangerous."

Taseu shrugged his shoulders. "But it doesn't exactly say there was a murder. It just says 'suspicious circumstances.'"

"But what do the police suspect?" Erana shivered. "There must be a reason."

"Or he might not have even been murdered but had an accident and got caught on the buoy," Toni said, then nodded, pleased to have found a less frightening solution. "Lots of people get lost during storms and things like that."

She stopped as Wiremu suddenly leaned forward, clenching his hands into fists as he usually did when he was determined to do something. "You know what, it really doesn't matter how he died. We still have to go to the island. We made a promise."

"That was before there was a body involved," Erana responded quickly.

"Forget the body! We decided that our group was going to be of service to people, and this is the first big project for the Coffin House Kids." Wiremu folded his arms as if the decision had been made. "Uncle Ammon has hurt himself pretty badly, and he's got to get the last crayfish catch done before the end of the season." He nodded thoughtfully. "And maybe while we're doing that, we can help solve the mystery about the body."

Toni glanced up just in time to see the twinkle in Wiremu's eyes as he waited for their reaction. Erana responded immediately as he knew she would.

"I'm not getting caught up with murderers! You're crazy, Wiremu." She shook her head adamantly so that the coil of thick, black hair swung loose over her shoulders. "No way!"

"But why not?" Wiremu winked at Toni as he leaned closer to his cousin and lowered his voice. "We have all the skills necessary to help with this investigation. "Toni's super-athletic, you're . . . well, you're really careful, and Taseu . . ."

"I'm fearless!" Taseu chuckled as he held up his hand, then winced as he rubbed his sore wrist. "Most of the time."

"Right, Taseu's fearless, and besides, nobody would suspect him of being a spy. He's a great decoy."

"A spy! Decoy?" Erana shook her head again. "You really are crazy. We're not spies! In fact, we're not even fishermen, so why are we going to the island in the first place?"

"Well, maybe not spies," Wiremu shrugged. "But—before I was rudely interrupted—Taseu's fearless and, well, I guess I'm the mastermind."

Even Toni had to suppress a giggle at this declaration. Wiremu seemed to have an amazing sense of self-esteem that simply didn't allow him to think he could fail at anything.

"Wiremu." Erana smiled patiently. "Everybody knows you have to have a mind to be a mastermind." She tapped her forehead knowingly. "I think you're missing something."

Taseu chuckled, and Toni snorted as Wiremu frowned. In a second they were all laughing, as Toni knew they would be. Even Rima gave a mellow, rumbling bark.

"Well, at least Rima will be with us on the island. She'll protect us." Toni patted the dog again.

"Mmm . . . she might not be that useful for fishing." Wiremu grinned, then he nodded thoughtfully. "But who knows what we might need her for once we get there."

* * *

Toni gently worked her fingers through the thick fur on Rima's neck as she sat at the window seat in her bedroom, staring through the nighttime darkness at the black silhouette of the cottage that had become known amongst their families as "the coffin house." At first she had been frightened of the cottage and the mysterious lights that had glowed at the attic window, but thanks to her friends, she had helped to uncover the mystery of the coffin house "ghost." There was nothing to fear now that she knew the cottage really belonged to Wiremu and Erana's Grandma Wini and that the "ghost" was a runaway boy.

"And I would never have met you and Jack if I hadn't gone into the cottage." Toni spoke quietly into Rima's ear, and the dog whined gently in response.

"Hi, chickie. Having trouble sleeping?"

Toni turned her head as her father spoke from the doorway.

"Hi, Dad." She smiled. "I was just thinking about our trip next week."

"Oh, I see." Professor Bradford leaned his tall body against the doorjamb, his hands in his jacket pockets. His glasses were propped on the top of his head as usual, like he was always ready to read something. "Are you worried about finding more bodies?"

"Not . . . really." Toni hesitated. "I mean, it's not likely is it?"

"Very unlikely, I would say." Her father frowned. "You know, you don't have to go to the island if you don't want to."

"Oh, but I do!" Toni responded quickly. "Since we became the Coffin House Kids, we decided we were going to try to be of service, and Wiremu says this is a big project for us." She shook her head. "His Uncle Ammon hurt his arm and leg pretty badly and he's got to get the last crayfish catch done. Wiremu reckons we'll be just the kind of help he needs."

Professor Bradford nodded slowly. It was good to see Toni overcoming her shyness as she spent time with Wiremu, Erana, and Taseu, and he was especially grateful that her friend Jack had given her Rima to look after while he was away at boarding school. All of these new friends helped to make up for the emptiness that had been left in their lives when Toni's mother had left them for good over two years ago.

"Well, I've had an idea." He stood up straight, and his tall frame seemed to fill the doorway. "Sandy is going to be on holiday as well, and I'd really like to come over and visit the island, so I think we might both come over on the weekend."

"Sandy . . . I mean, Miss Jenson?" Toni nodded slowly. She was still getting used to her father's growing friendship with the American relief teacher who was also her basketball coach. She nodded thoughtfully. "That would be good."

"Mmmmm, I thought so." Professor Bradford smiled happily. "It will give us all a chance to spend some time together, and besides, you can't get into too much trouble in four days."

CHAPTER TWO

The early-morning sun was already hot as it rose up across the harbor and shone relentlessly onto the lines of people standing on the dock. Boats of various shapes and sizes, from smaller ferries to huge ocean liners, lined up along the heavy wooden sidings of the Auckland wharves, their painted steel hulls rubbing against the timber as tiny waves effortlessly moved their bulk. Circling seagulls cried out harshly before landing on posts and staring inquisitively at all the people carrying bags or shuffling them along with their feet as they moved in line. The four children made their way past the glass-fronted ticket offices and cobbled pathway that led out onto the dock.

"Did you remember your snorkel?" Erana asked as she turned suddenly to Wiremu. Her shoulder-length black hair was tied in tight braids that whipped into his face as he followed closely behind her. "And flippers?"

"Pah!" Wiremu blinked the hair from his eyes and frowned. "Of course I've got them. We're going to an island with water and swimming. I packed them first."

"Which means you probably left something else out." Erana shrugged. "Grandma said you would. I was just checking."

"I must have repacked about four times." Toni eased her bag off her shoulder and kept a tight hold on Rima's leash. "I think I have far too much stuff."

"Well, Uncle Ammon said we'd only need old clothes to work in and things to swim in." Wiremu nodded importantly. "It's not a fashion parade on the island."

"Did you mean it when you said there wasn't a shop there?" Taseu looked concerned as he glanced back toward a small restaurant shop selling delicious-smelling pastries. He patted his stomach without thinking. "Do you think I should have brought more supplies?"

"There are shops on the main island, but we're going to the little island where Uncle Ammon lives, and there aren't any shops or roads there. Our cousin Jerry said there'll be plenty to eat though." He paused and looked thoughtful. "It's going to be funny to see Jerry again. I haven't seen him since we were about seven years old."

"Is he much like you?" Taseu asked with one eyebrow raised.

"He's smaller than me." Wiremu nodded confidently. "I used to beat him in races and things."

"That was five years ago," Erana interrupted. "And Grandma says he'd changed a lot when she saw him last year."

"Well, I reckon I'll still be able to beat him, though." Wiremu grinned and flexed his arm to show some muscle. "Anyway, we'll all see soon enough. There'll be plenty of physical-type challenges on the island."

"It sounds like it'll be so much fun." Toni was enthusiastic. "I reckon Rima will love it."

"Do you think Miss Jenson will like it when she comes over?" Erana strained up on her tiptoes to look through the crowd. "She's used to life in the city."

"But she said she used to do trips up into the mountains back home in Utah." Toni waved out to the tall woman working her way through the lines toward them.

"It's all outdoorsy things."

"She'll like anything," Wiremu stated confidently. "Miss Jenson is just like that. I think it's great that she'll be coming over with your dad."

"I'll say," Taseu agreed, then frowned. "Although I can't believe I'm saying that about a teacher."

"It's like she's not really a teacher." Toni switched hands on Rima's leash. "She's more our basketball coach than our teacher. And it's only a few more weeks before she goes back to America."

"She's your dad's girlfriend," Wiremu whispered and watched with a satisfied smile as the color instantly rose in Toni's cheeks. "Not that any of us are complaining. And it's really nice of her to bring us over to the ferry. Grandma hates the city traffic."

They stopped talking as they were ushered slowly forward by the ferry deckhands loading bags into large cages. As each cage filled up, they sealed it and put it into a lift that was lowered down into the boat.

"See, Rima?" Wiremu knelt down beside the dog and pointed to the disappearing cage. "That's where you have to go—down with the cargo."

Rima shifted restlessly and made a soft, whining noise in her throat as she backed up against Toni.

"Wiremu, that's mean!" Toni patted the dog's head reassuringly and shook her head at Wiremu. "It's okay, Rima. We're not going to put you down there, but the skipper said you'll have to stay out on the deck."

"And we'll put Wiremu down with the bags," Erana suggested happily. "Then we can all have a pleasant trip."

They all laughed as Wiremu pulled her braid, then they began to move their bags toward the cage as the deckhand directed them.

"Wow, just in time!" Sandy Jenson eased past the edge of the cage. Her long, blonde hair was tied back in a ponytail, and a blue sports cap was set firmly on top of her head. "The line at the ticket office was really long. I think everybody is going to Great Barrier for the holiday." She fanned out some tickets in her hand. "Everybody take one."

Wiremu nodded as he took his ticket. "My uncle said it's been really busy, but we won't have to worry about tourists on the island."

"*Our* uncle," Erana corrected him brightly. "And our cousin Jerry said there'll be heaps to do as well as just the crayfishing."

"Now a crayfish is what I'd call a lobster in America, right?" Sandy crooked an eyebrow. "I didn't know what you meant at first."

"Yep." Wiremu nodded importantly. "But Rock Lobsters, not the big lobsters with the big pincer things." He made a snapping motion with two fingers. "It's just that we call them crayfish in New Zealand."

"I get it." Sandy rested her hand on Rima's head as she glanced toward the boat. "I'm looking forward to coming out on the weekend, and, seeing as how

I'll be there as a friend and I will be leaving soon, how about we forget that I'm Miss Jenson or Sister Jenson while we're away and you all just call me Sandy?"

The children all looked at each other quickly, and then Taseu beamed. "Sounds great, Sandy!" Just the sound of her name coming from his own lips made him put his hand to his mouth as his dark brown eyes grew wide. "Wow, did I say that?"

Wiremu pretended to ponder, then he nodded thoughtfully. "I think that's a good idea . . . Sandy."

Toni stood quietly as the other three tried saying it in different tones while their coach laughed happily. Toni had been trying hard to get used to using "Sister Jenson" at home and at church and "Miss Jenson" at school, and then when her father started referring to her as "Sandy," Toni had felt very uncertain about which name she should use. This official permission to use Sandy's first name was almost a relief, and yet . . . she wasn't sure if she wanted to be too personal.

They waited a few more minutes while their bags were loaded, the boat rocking slowly up and down with the movement of the waves.

"I wonder how rough it will get out at sea." Toni frowned as she watched the boat move. "I haven't been on a boat since I was really tiny— before we went to live in Australia."

"Really?" Miss Jenson looked surprised. "I mean, I thought you were born in Australia."

"No." Toni shook her head. "I was born down near Hamilton, and we moved to Australia when I was four. Dad and I came back to Auckland about the same time you came here."

"And we got a new coach and a tall center for our basketball team in one hit," Wiremu joined in beside them. "I believe in divine intervention."

"So do I." Erana was right beside him. "Otherwise, Wiremu would have tried to be everything on the basketball team—especially the coach."

"Well, I can't believe it's just about time for me to go home again." Miss Jenson took a deep breath. "I'm finding I really don't want to leave my Warriors."

Toni twisted her hair into a ponytail as she thought about their coach leaving. Miss Jenson had been much more than a coach in the time she'd been at their school. When they had discovered that she was a member of their church as well, she had become a friend of all their families. She had helped Wiremu and Erana when their grandmother was ill, she'd given Taseu and his brother extra tutoring, and then—Toni gulped. Then there had been the steadily growing relationship between

Miss Jenson and her own father. Apart from sitting with Toni and her father in church and attending ward activities together, Miss Jenson had gone on several dates with Professor Bradford over the last few weeks. Toni had noticed her father's increasingly happy attitude and how much he had been humming songs as he worked at home. She wasn't sure how close her father and Sandy were getting, and she really wasn't sure how to deal with it.

"Well, I'm sure we can find a way to keep you here." Wiremu looked thoughtful. "We'll have to deal with it when we get back from the island."

"That would be nice, Wiremu." Sandy grinned at his confidence. "I'll look forward to that."

Just as she spoke, the deckhand began to motion them to come on board, and the children carefully made their way along the gangplank and onto the boat, waving back at Miss Jenson.

"We have to take Rima straight outside." Toni pointed toward the side of the boat. "Or out the back."

"Let's go out the side." Erana was already leading the way. "Jerry said we might even see dolphins or whales racing the boat once we get out into the gulf."

"Dolphins?" Toni looked up quickly. "Real dolphins?"

"No, inflatable ones." Taseu didn't even crack a smile for at least a second before he giggled, his round cheeks making his eyes into slits. "Wouldn't that be so funny . . . a bunch of inflatable dolphins."

"Not even funny." Wiremu punched him gently. "But I wouldn't mind seeing a whale. Now that would be really awesome."

Within twenty minutes all the passengers were on board, and the ferry slowly pulled away from the wharf and eased out into Waitemata Harbour. The tall, slender needle of the Sky Tower—the topmost pinnacle of the city skyline—faded into the distance as they left the land behind, and soon the children were watching yachts cutting deftly through the water beside them as the boat cruised up the channel.

* * *

"I never realized there was so much water." Wiremu shaded his eyes with his hand. "Just lots of blue water and blue sky."

"And we're still only in the gulf." Erana pointed at some tiny rocky outcrops pointing upward in the sea. "Look, there's land."

"That's not land." Taseu squinted. "That's just a seagull stopover."

"Well, I'm tired of looking at water." Erana shrugged. "I'm going to sit inside and read. I don't think we're going to see any fish."

"Dolphins aren't fish—they're mammals." Wiremu frowned. "And the hostess lady said they almost always spot them, so I'm staying here. You too, eh, Toni?"

Toni nodded and stroked Rima's head. "I'm happy here."

"I think I'll go with Erana." Taseu eased past them. "I want to watch the skipper through that little window in the door."

Wiremu and Toni stayed leaning against the rail, watching the frothing white wake wash up the side as the boat churned through the dark blue-green ocean.

"It looks so dark. It's almost scary if you think how deep it is." Toni frowned as she peered harder into the water. "It's clear, but it's dark. I doubt if we could see the dolphins anyway."

"You'll see them." A deep voice spoke behind her shoulder, and Toni and Wiremu both jumped a little as they turned quickly. "If the dolphins can hear the boat, they'll come."

The man was very tall. He had to stoop slightly as he stepped out onto the platform beside them, and his broad shoulders seemed to fill the width of the narrow doorway. He was wearing very dark glasses so they couldn't see his eyes, and his hands were sunk deeply into the pockets of his water-proof jacket.

Rima emitted a low, deep growl as he stepped out onto the narrow pathway beside them, and Toni tightened her grip on the dog's collar. The man's jaw tightened, and a long, thin scar running the length of his jawline pulsed. He took a step back against the boat while Toni maneuvered Rima away from him.

"Have you seen them before?" Wiremu was not the least bit shy. "Out here?"

"A few times." The man nodded toward the water. "And usually around about here."

"Truly?" Toni deliberately looked back at the water, trying to ignore the man's scar. "I'd love to see some."

As if by magic, the water at the side of the boat was suddenly alive with long, gray shapes, lifting and diving with the movement of the boat's wake. Toni and Wiremu watched in awestruck silence as the dolphins kept pace with the boat, occasionally dropping out of sight only to resurface farther out, soaring out of the water and dropping in graceful dives.

"Oh, they're so beautiful." Toni barely breathed the words as her hands gripped the rail. "Oh, my goodness, there's a little baby one."

They leaned out farther to watch as a smaller dolphin swam close to the boat. Then out of nowhere a much larger one surfaced between the baby and the boat and nosed it away.

"That'll be its mother," the stranger observed almost in a whisper, his voice deep and low. "She'll be trying to protect her baby from getting too inquisitive about the boat."

"Really?" Toni looked up. "But what about those? They don't look much bigger and they're really close." She pointed to several slightly larger dolphins that were rising and falling right in the path of the ferry.

"Those are the teenage males." The stranger barely smiled. "They just want to get close to the danger. Sometimes they don't learn quickly enough . . . and they pay the price."

There was a long silence that suddenly felt uncomfortable, and Toni began to wish the stranger hadn't joined them. She could feel that Rima was still tense as well.

"Are you a scientist?" Wiremu suddenly stared at the stranger with his head to one side. "You know a lot."

The man shook his head while seeming to keep his face averted. "Not a scientist—just interested . . . in a lot of things. Dolphins are fascinating animals."

There was another long silence, then Wiremu frowned. "It's a pity there weren't any dolphins around to protect that man that was killed out at the island," Wiremu remarked casually as he stared out at the dolphins, but Toni noticed that the man's jaw clenched again and that he swallowed hard.

"Oh, what man was that?" The stranger raised an eyebrow above the dark lens of his glasses.

"I don't know him personally." Wiremu shrugged and screwed up his nose. "Some guy they found caught on some crayfish lines. They reckon someone killed him." He grasped the metal rail and leaned back confidently. "We're going out to help our uncle with his crayfishing, so we'll probably have to help with the investigation."

Toni stared at Wiremu wide-eyed, shocked at his boldness, then she suddenly noticed that the stranger seemed even more disconcerted. The scar on his jaw pulsed as he cleared his throat.

"Um . . . you seem a bit young to help with the investigation of a possible murder. That could be dangerous."

"Not really." Wiremu nodded knowingly. "After all, who would suspect a group of kids of being detectives . . ." He stopped as he noticed the look on Toni's face and realized he'd probably said too much. "So, anyway . . . are you going fishing over there?"

The stranger hesitated slightly, then shook his head. "No, I'm not really interested in fishing." He stared out at the water for a moment. "You say your uncle's a fisherman? Do you mean he likes fishing?"

"Oh, no." Wiremu straightened his shoulders as he sensed the man's interest. "He's a real fisherman . . . like, that's his full-time job. He mainly does crayfishing and mussel farming."

"You said you're going to help him?"

"That's because he broke his arm, and he needs deckhands because he can only drive the boat. My cousin Jerry is there, but they need our help as well," Wiremu finished seriously.

"Oh, I see." The man nodded slowly. "Do you know what you're going to be doing?"

Wiremu's eyes flickered uncertainly toward Toni, then he shrugged.

"Being deckhands, of course. Helping catch crayfish."

Toni thought she saw the faintest smile twitch at the corner of the man's mouth, then he pursed his lips, and a slight frown appeared on his forehead. "Do you know where you'll be fishing?"

Again Wiremu hesitated, then he nodded his head more definitely.

"Out this side of the big island—among the little islands." His face brightened as he recalled more. "My uncle's been fishing there for years, and he's got over a hundred pots. Way over a hundred—maybe two hundred," he added dramatically, and Toni looked at him quickly. Grandma Wini had said about a hundred. Wiremu was such an exaggerator.

"Two hundred?" The man's eyebrows raised slightly. "That must take a lot of looking after."

"That's why he needs our help." Wiremu folded his arms knowingly. "We have to help him get things done before the season finishes."

Toni watched as the man again nodded slowly. For someone who wasn't interested in fishing, it seemed to her that he was showing more than a passing interest in Wiremu's information. She suddenly felt uncomfortable with his questions and deliberately pulled on Wiremu's sleeve and pointed toward the water. "Look, they're moving away."

The dolphins were dropping out of sight, one by one, their steel-gray bodies blending in with the dark blue depths. Within seconds, Taseu was at the doorway with Erana close behind.

"Did you see them? Weren't they awesome?" Taseu's eyes were wide as he made diving motions with his hand.

"We saw heaps, and he . . ." Wiremu hesitated as he looked at the man, not knowing what to call him. "He told us all about them."

The man suddenly looked preoccupied as he stared hard beyond the other two standing in the doorway. Then with an abrupt nod, he moved quickly past them, forcing Erana against the side of the cabin. "Have fun fishing," the man mumbled, and then he disappeared into the crowd of people that was passing by the entrance to the small on-board café.

There was a brief silence as they all turned, then Wiremu shrugged. "I guess he needed to go to the bathroom or something."

"He was sure in a hurry." Erana rubbed her arm where the man had pushed against her. "He didn't have to be rude, though."

Toni frowned at the doorway then back at her friends. "He was actually quite nice before you got here, except . . ." She hesitated and glanced at Wiremu. "Did you notice how many questions he was asking about your uncle?"

"No, not really." Wiremu shook his head. "I think he was just surprised that I knew so much about fishing."

"Like the two hundred cray pots?" Toni couldn't help smiling.

"Two hundred!" Erana looked puzzled. "Grandma said about a hundred. Weren't you listening?"

"Well, yes, but . . ." Wiremu actually looked embarrassed, then his face brightened. "One hundred, two hundred, what does it matter? It's not like it means anything to anyone."

Taseu took a turn staying with Rima while Toni, Erana, and Wiremu went to sit inside for a while. It was much warmer inside the cabin, especially where the sun beat through the thick panelled glass. Wiremu sat opposite Toni and Erana at one of the tables.

"That was a bonus seeing the dolphins, wasn't it?" Wiremu took a bite of a sandwich. "They were amazing."

Toni nodded enthusiastically. "They were so beautiful! And Erana, did you see the mother with her baby? The man said she looks after the baby so it won't get hurt by the boat, and he was right. I saw her pushing the baby away with her nose and her body." She shook her head. "I had no idea they did that."

Erana nodded wisely. "A mother's natural instinct is to look after her baby. A book I was reading said dolphins are very protective."

"That's what the man said." Toni frowned slightly. "I think my mother must be an exception."

Wiremu sat quietly. He knew Toni's mother had suddenly run out on Toni and her father two years before, leaving them for another man without so much as a backward glance. He also knew how much Professor Bradford cared about his daughter.

"Yeah, but I don't think dolphins have dads like yours that can look after their daughters."

Toni nodded slowly.

"No, I guess they don't." She smiled briefly, liking the way Wiremu seemed to understand how she felt. "I guess I'm glad my dad's not a dolphin."

There was a brief silence, then Erana gestured with her hand toward the deck. "So, who was that man with all the information about dolphins? Was he friendly? Because he didn't look like it when I came out."

Toni bit at her bottom lip as she thought about the conversation they'd had. "I wouldn't say friendly. He just told us about the dolphins, but then when you came out . . . I don't know why he left so quickly." She frowned. "It was almost like he was scared or something."

"Scared of Taseu and Erana?" Wiremu looked doubtful. "I could understand being scared of Erana, but Taseu . . . ?"

"No, no, he seemed to see something inside, then he just rushed off." Toni shook her head. "It was a bit weird."

"Oh well, it's not like you'll have to worry about him anymore." Erana lifted up her book to read and deliberately turned her shoulder toward Wiremu. "Now if you'll excuse me, I'll keep reading so I don't scare anybody else."

* * *

The ferry docked at Tryphena, and many of the passengers got off. But the children stayed on board, hanging over the rails and watching the deckhands unload the luggage. The children waved to some of the passengers making their way onto the wharf.

Taseu looked around as the final cage of baggage was lifted ashore. "We're practically the only ones left." He looked at Wiremu. "Where are we going?"

"Port Fitzroy." Erana answered first. "And Uncle Ammon is going to meet us there with Jerry. They'll take us back to the island in their boat."

"Another boat?" Taseu rolled his eyes and rubbed his stomach as if it was churning. "So much water and so many boats."

"You should be fine with water and boats— you're a Polynesian from the 'isles of the sea.'" Wiremu teased. "You've just lived in the city too long."

"Hey, did anyone notice that man getting off?" Toni suddenly interrupted as she scanned the waterfront.

"You mean the 'dolphin man'?" Wiremu glanced back at the wharf as the boat began to move away. "I didn't really notice. Maybe he got off quickly."

"Very quickly." Toni frowned slightly. "He was so tall you'd have thought he would have stood out in the crowd, but I never saw him."

"The way he took off when he knocked me over, I don't think he wanted to be noticed." Erana observed primly, tossing her hair back. "I still think he was a bit rude."

"Maybe he wanted to get on holiday quickly." Wiremu shaded his eyes with his hand as he watched the road leading away from the wharf. "You know, when I think about it, he seemed to know a lot about the dolphins and the island, but he didn't even know about the body."

"What body?" Erana glanced at him, then she nodded. "Oh . . . the body on the buoy. Why did you talk about that?"

"It changed the subject from Uncle Ammon's two hundred crayfish pots." Toni grinned again.

"Are you sure that wasn't three hundred?" Taseu chuckled as he shook his head. "Man, we are going to be so busy with all those pots."

"Okay, you guys, so I exaggerated a little." Wiremu grinned, not looking the least bit remorseful as he shrugged his shoulders. "Besides, what does it matter what Dolphin Man thinks or knows about crayfish pots?"

"Ah, but he may be an evil crayfish poacher in disguise." Taseu lowered his voice and glanced over his shoulder as if someone might be listening. "He might be watching us even now so that we'll lead him to a crayfish treasure."

"Don't be an idiot." Wiremu thumped him lightly on the arm as Taseu laughed again. "He was just interested in what I was telling him."

"Well, I guess if he were to go looking for two hundred pots he'd be disappointed, wouldn't he?" Erana rolled her eyes expressively to show she was tired of the conversation. "Anyway, let's forget about him. Where do you think our island is?"

The subject of the disappearing dolphin man was forgotten as the boat made its way out of the sheltered harbor and northwards up the rugged coastline. They passed sheltered bays with boats of all sizes moored offshore, and in between, craggy gray cliffs rose sharply from the water, intersected with acres of dense green native bush and trees that often reached right to the water's edge.

Then the boat threaded its way down through a channel guarded on both sides by small, rocky islands. One or two islands were noticeably bigger and showed signs of having people living on them, but there was no sign of any roads or cars.

Wiremu studied one small settlement as the boat forged past, and then he turned thoughtfully. "I think it must be one of these islands we'll be staying on." He squinted in the bright sunlight. "I wish I knew which one."

CHAPTER THREE

"Look, there's Uncle Ammon!" Erana was the first to spot the man in a small fishing boat making its way past several larger yachts anchored in the narrow harbor of Port Fitzroy. She waved, then waited impatiently with the others on the edge of the wharf as the boat drew up to the wooden moorings. "Hi, Uncle Ammon!"

"Hey, kids!" The top of Ammon Ammon's face was shaded by a wide-brimmed straw hat as he waved back from where he was steering the boat, but Toni recognized the broad grin that was so like Erana's and Wiremu's.

They waited as the boat pulled in close to the wharf. A young boy came out of the cabin and reached up to quickly secure a rope around one of the upright posts.

"So, you all got here in one piece!" Uncle Ammon spoke loudly as he stopped the engine and stepped out onto the deck. His left arm, supported in a sling, was encased in a heavy plaster cast from his hand to his armpit, but he rested his good hand on his son's shoulder. "Do you think you can keep this lot under control for the next few days, Jerry?"

"No problem." Jerry grinned, his white teeth contrasting with his pale brown skin. He was wearing a sleeveless shirt, and his arms were tanned a deep brown from the summer sun. Even though he looked to be about twelve, he was at least three inches taller than Wiremu, and the firm muscles on his arms showed that he did a lot of physical work. "We'll just keep everybody working hard."

He grinned again, and Toni stared at Jerry then back at Wiremu. She'd always thought that Erana and Wiremu were similar, but there was definitely a family likeness here as well, almost as if the two boys could be brothers. She suppressed a giggle. Two Wiremus! This could be a really interesting holiday.

Uncle Ammon grinned. "So, who have you brought to help you, Wiremu?" "Introduce me to my new deckhands."

"Okay." Wiremu nodded importantly. "Well, you know Erana will be the cook, of course, and this is Taseu Ta'ala. He loves engines and stuff, so he'll probably want to help drive the boat. And this is Toni Bradford. She wants to be a marine biologist, so she'll probably want to throw all the fish back so they don't get hurt, but she's really strong."

Uncle Ammon gave a hearty laugh at the descriptions as he glanced at Jerry. "And then there's Wiremu, who'll want to catch the whole quota of crayfish on his own."

They all laughed at Uncle Ammon's very accurate description of Wiremu, and Toni felt a warm rush of happiness as she contemplated spending the next few days with him and her friends. This was going to be an exciting holiday!

The fishing boat was a sturdy wooden vessel with a small cabin and narrow seating. Although clean, it had an undeniable fishy smell that seemed to linger in the hot, noonday sun.

"Phew!" Taseu pinched his nose with two fingers. "We're definitely not on a farm."

"Wait till we get the fish on board." Uncle Ammon laughed again and nudged Jerry, who was standing beside them. "I think these 'townies' have a bit to learn, don't you?"

Jerry grinned and nodded without speaking, and Toni suddenly realized that his appearance was where his likeness to Wiremu ended. Wiremu had an opinion on most things and liked to share, whereas she felt that Jerry would think a lot more before he actually spoke.

Uncle Ammon kept the boat at a slow pace as they threaded their way past a few pristine white boats with blue and red nautical trims and headed out toward the open sea. The children all sat quietly, holding onto the sides of the boat or the railing. The water was much closer to them in this smaller boat than on the large tri-level catamaran they had just been on, and the wash of water came up the sides.

"I'm glad it's not too rough," Toni whispered to Erana and received a brief nod in response. "Are you scared?"

"Not scared." Erana's eyes grew wide as the boat suddenly picked up speed. "But I think I'm really a 'land person.'"

The back of the boat sunk slightly lower in the water as they made their way up a channel toward a cluster of large rocks, and the waves became much more definite as the boat rose and fell with each new swell.

"Just imagine you're riding a horse." Uncle Ammon glanced at their faces from where he stood behind the steering wheel. "Rise and fall with the movement, and you'll get your sea legs pretty soon."

"I've forgotten how my land legs feel," Erana groaned. "Right now I feel like I've got sea stomach."

Her uncle grinned and slowed the boat slightly. "You'll get used to it. We'll have you out every day, and you'll be a real sailor in no time."

"I think I'd rather be your stay-at-home cook." Erana put her hand to her mouth. "I was all right on the ferry. It felt like a big house. This is just so close to the water."

Wiremu was beginning to get used to the rolling movement of the boat and even ventured to stand up and pretend to be surfing the waves. "It's actually a good feeling when you get used to it." He looked at Jerry, who was standing quite calmly, almost as if there was no motion. "I reckon it'd be great to have some really big waves."

"What are the biggest waves you've been in, Jerry?" Taseu kept a firm grip on the edge of the boat, his sturdy legs braced firmly apart.

"Oh, reasonably big," Jerry answered quietly. "It's not a good idea to go out if they're too big."

"But what's the biggest?" Taseu persisted. "Were they crashing over the boat? Were you scared?"

Jerry glanced at his father, then he shrugged.

"I wasn't scared because I was with Dad, but we got caught out in the channel with a sudden wind change. The waves would've been about nine feet, so they were crashing over the boat pretty hard."

Toni felt her stomach sink at the thought, and she tried to smile. "We won't be doing that will we?" Her voice broke a little, and Jerry smiled back.

"No, Dad won't take anyone out if it's too rough. You'll be safe."

"Hey, that reminds me, speaking of safe . . . or not safe." Wiremu held his hand up to his eyes as he squinted against the sunlight. "Do you know where they found that body the other day—the guy that was tied to the buoy? Was it around here?"

There was a long silence, and Toni noticed how Jerry's eyes flickered immediately toward his father. He hesitated before answering with a brief nod and a gesture to their right.

"Dad said it was somewhere out that way." Jerry swallowed hard. "I don't know much about it."

"But it was on the front page of the newspaper." Erana frowned. "Didn't you see it?"

"I don't get much time to read the paper," Jerry answered quietly but firmly, and Toni noticed his jaw tighten. It was obvious Jerry didn't want to discuss the discovery of the man's body.

"But imagine if you had pulled him out of the water." Taseu's eyes widened, and he made a pulling motion with his hand. "Imagine finding that on the end of the line!"

"There's plenty to do around here without having to use your imagination." Jerry turned abruptly and swung himself up onto the top of the boat cabin. "Anyone want a better view of the island?"

Toni stood quietly as both Wiremu and Taseu were distracted at once and attempted to follow him up. Then she frowned slightly as she shielded her eyes and stared in the direction Jerry had indicated. The waves rose and fell in smooth green rounds, and she could only see one tiny white boat far away in the distance. But a sudden thought seemed to fill her mind, and a shiver ran down her back. There was nothing much to see on top of the water, but what were they going to encounter in the depths underneath the rolling waves?

* * *

There really weren't any roads on the island where they finally pulled in. There were just a few houses, and the only sign of life was a dog pacing up and down the wooden jetty. Rima immediately tensed and began to whimper and strain at her lead, but Toni held her firmly.

Jerry gently stroked Rima's head. "It's okay; you'll be fine with Miner. He only gets upset if a male dog comes on his territory." Toni had been sure to introduce Jerry and Rima properly as soon as they had gotten on the boat, and Rima seemed very content to sit quietly while he soothed her.

Now Toni recognized that the tone of his voice was very similar to Jack's, Rima's owner.

"I think you remind her of her owner, Jack Thompson," Toni offered shyly. "You sound a bit like him."

"Her owner?" Jerry frowned. "Isn't she yours?"

"Well, sort of." Toni hesitated. "She belongs to our friend Jack, but he's gone down to board at Church College, so—I was sort of scared of dogs until I met Rima—so Jack said I could look after her while he's away, and now she sort of looks after me."

"Sort of." Jerry grinned as he copied her, and she felt her cheeks burn. He was even teasing her like Jack did.

"Actually, Rima is just like one of the team," Wiremu suddenly interrupted from behind them. "It's like she belongs to all of us."

"Well, I'm sure Miner will enjoy getting to know her," Jerry answered quietly. "Although she's a lot bigger than he is."

"That's not a problem," Taseu chimed in cheerfully. "We're used to girls being bigger than us. Look at Toni. She's way bigger."

In that instant, Toni became very aware of standing several inches taller than Wiremu or Taseu, and she immediately bent lower to straighten Rima's collar even though it didn't need straightening. She had finally gotten used to being "the tall girl," but sometimes it was painful to be reminded of how tall she was.

"Hey, it's not just about height," Erana chimed in quickly. "Sometimes you just get tired of waiting for the boys to catch up. I'm always waiting for Wiremu."

Once again Toni marvelled at how the cousins could tease each other without taking offense. Even now they were laughing together, and she realized how fortunate she was to have them as her friends, not just at school but at church as well.

* * *

"Okay now, the girls are in the small holiday cottage out back, and all of the boys are in the room down the hallway." Ammon pointed with both hands. "We'll have lunch ready in ten minutes, then Jerry can show you around the island."

"Are we going to work today?" Wiremu swung his bag over his shoulder, narrowly missing Taseu, who was standing right behind him. "Should we get changed?"

"We already did a few pots this morning before you got here. I think we'll just let you relax and have a look around and a swim today." Uncle

Ammon smiled. "But you better be up bright and early in the morning. We'll be lifting about thirty pots tomorrow."

As the boys filed down to their room, the girls made their way out to the cottage. It was really just a large room with a tiny bathroom and very little decoration apart from two single beds with multi-striped duvets, a few green striped towels, and some blue striped curtains at the window.

"I'm glad I like stripes." Erana glanced around before she put her bag beside one of the beds and yawned. "My goodness, it's still only afternoon, but after all that salt air, I'm already sleepy."

"I think a swim sounds like a good idea." Toni put her bag on the other bed and unzipped it. "I am really, really hot, especially since we got onto dry land, and I think Rima will enjoy a swim as well. She was panting so hard."

"So would you if you ran around like she did when she met Miner. They were like long-lost friends." Erana giggled. "I think Rima's got a boyfriend already."

They heard the boys outside almost immediately, so the girls quickly changed into their swimsuits with their long beach shorts and T-shirts on top and joined them at the long wooden table. Jerry was cutting chunky slices from a large loaf of homemade bread, and Uncle Ammon had several containers of butter, jam, savory vegemite spread, and peanut butter arranged along his plaster cast as he carried them to the table.

"There's got to be some advantages to having a broken arm." He smiled broadly as he put all the containers down. "But this is the only one I've found so far."

"I think you manage very well." Erana nodded primly as she glanced around at some piles of dirty dishes. "But I can see why you need our help."

Toni watched Jerry exchange a look with his father, and they both smiled. Erana loved to organize people, and she especially liked having the house neat and tidy.

"Well, I reckon you can just tidy things to your heart's content, my girl." Uncle Ammon playfully tousled Erana's hair. "I'm sure you'll have us all organized by the end of the day, and old Auntie Mere is over at the other house if you need anything. She's so old she can't really move around too well, but she'll love having company. We all will." He stopped, then he cleared his throat. "I want to say how much I appreciate you all coming over to help us out like this. When my wife had to go stay with her mother because she was so ill, and then I had this accident, and the guy who usually helps me had just gone overseas . . . well, I knew I could rely on Jerry to do a lot, but I really didn't know what to do." He stopped and ran his hand through his hair almost as if he were embarrassed. "It was Jerry who suggested we pray about it, and afterward—well, almost straight afterward, he remembered my telling him stories about how Erana's father used to come over here and help when he was a teenager."

"And now we're nearly teenagers, and we just happened to be on holiday." Wiremu flexed his muscles as he took up the story. "And we could help as well."

Uncle Ammon laughed. "Well, I don't want to spoil your holiday by making you work all the time. You need to have some time to explore and have fun. With his sisters all grown up and gone to work in town, Jerry usually only has old Miner to talk to, so it's good for him to have company as well."

Toni glanced at Jerry. Upon arriving at the island, she had been impressed with how exciting the place looked with its wild rockiness and the ocean surrounding it. Suddenly she realized how lonely it must be for Jerry to be the only kid here. How did he go to school or church? Where did he go to have fun?

"I like it," Jerry responded quietly, as if in answer to her silent questions. "I've got heaps to do, and Miner's a good listener. He always wants to do what I want."

"Just like Rima," Toni put in quickly. "I'm never lonely now." She glanced around at her friends. "I mean, I'm not lonely with all of you, but it's nice to have company at home." She rolled her eyes. "I mean, I know what you mean, Jerry. Dogs are great friends."

At that moment, Miner suddenly barked loudly, making everyone jump except Jerry and his father. Rima sat up quickly and joined in, but it was as if she just wanted to make noise as well.

"That'll be a new boat coming past." Uncle Ammon crooked his thumb toward the ocean. "Miner has a different bark for different boats. If it's one he knows, his bark is kind of mellow and welcoming, but if it's a stranger, it's louder and more persistent, like a challenge, until the boat goes past." He watched as both dogs raised themselves off the veranda and started down the path to the wharf, still barking. "We must have a new visitor coming in."

Uncle Ammon walked to the door, and they all rose from the table and followed. From the top of the path, they could see the dogs standing on the wharf watching a very large launch resting out in the channel. The sun was reflecting brightly off the stainless steel fittings and railings that surrounded the sleek, white sides. The engine was idling at a low hum, but the launch wasn't moving.

"It must be a very rich holiday-maker, ready to do a lot of fishing." Uncle Ammon summed up the splendid appearance of the yacht, complete with fishing rods ready to use on the back deck.

"Mmm, must be." Jerry raised his hand to shield his eyes from the sun and studied the boat closely. "Do you think they want some crayfish, Dad?" Jerry looked at his father. "Shall I row out?"

"No . . . no, don't worry." Uncle Ammon suddenly turned away quickly. "They'll come in if they want us." He began to walk back to the house, then saw the confused looks on the children's faces and paused to explain. "We're right at the top of the channel here, so we're the first contact on the Barrier. The locals sometimes tell people we have crayfish to sell."

"Do you sell many?" Wiremu stared back at the boat.

"A few." Uncle Ammon started walking again. "The honest ones buy them off us—others just help themselves out of the pots."

"Like poachers?" Wiremu picked up on his uncle's words immediately as he followed behind him. "Like that guy whose body was found?"

Uncle Ammon stopped walking. "That had nothing to do with us." His voice was quietly firm. "The man wasn't a poacher—the newspapers just got carried away with a story."

"So he wasn't a poacher?" Wiremu sounded faintly disappointed. "We thought we might be able to help you catch them—the poachers, that is—or the murderers."

"Wiremu, you're here to help us with fishing and to have a holiday. That's it, okay?" Uncle Ammon's voice had lost its normal joking tone, and he glanced quickly back toward the yacht.

"Uh . . . sure." Wiremu nodded slowly. "I just thought—"

"Don't think about anything other than enjoying yourself." Uncle Ammon suddenly grinned to lighten the mood. "Oh, and working hard of course. Now, let's get that lunch finished."

Toni lagged slightly behind as the others made their way back to the house, all chattering happily. She was slightly confused by Uncle Ammon's response to the talk about the poachers, and then there was his reaction to the boat moored out in the channel. He had seemed surprised to see it and had studied it very carefully at first. Then all of a sudden he had turned away from it, as if to stop them all from looking. She turned back to look at the yacht once more.

There hadn't been any movement on the boat when they had walked down the jetty, but now she was sure she'd seen a figure come up into the cabin and then quickly disappear again—a tall figure wearing very dark glasses and a pale beige jacket.

"Exactly like the dolphin man," she half-whispered to Rima as she squinted for a better look. "But why would he be on a fishing boat when he said he wasn't interested in fishing?"

"Toni!" Taseu stopped to call her. "Come and have lunch so we can explore!"

"Right!" She turned her head briefly to answer, and when she looked back there was no one in the boat. She shook her head as if to shake out the thought. "There are lots of tall people in the world."

CHAPTER FOUR

"How far is it?" Taseu panted slightly as he side-stepped over some long strands of grass while Rima and Miner walked in front of him.

"Just over the hill." Jerry pointed toward a tall knoll to their left, topped with several large, gray rocks that seemed almost completely round.

"That's not a hill!" Taseu stopped in his tracks to wipe the perspiration off his forehead. "That's almost vertical!"

They all laughed at the expression on his face, then Jerry pointed in the other direction. "Just kidding. We're going to the bay around the side of the hill. It's flat." He kept walking. "We'll go up that one tomorrow morning before breakfast."

"Before breakfast?" Taseu took a deep breath, and Toni could hear him muttering as he hurried up behind her. "I thought we were having a holiday. This is going to be like Camp Punishment."

"I think he's joking." She smiled. Taseu always grumbled about physical exercise, and yet he was

one of the strongest boys she knew. It was strange
how he could be a combination of strong and gen-
tle. She always felt safe with Taseu around, and she
loved how he made her laugh.

They kept walking through the long grass,
which had been yellowed by the brilliant summer
sun and brisk ocean winds. The dogs seemed to
love the excursion, first following the path with
the children, then suddenly leaping away and bur-
rowing through the long grass with only their
haunches showing. Even when they stopped, panting loudly with their mouths open and tongues
out, they seemed to be laughing with enjoyment.

"I wonder how digging through itchy grass
with your nose can be fun." Erana screwed up her
nose and rubbed it. "It must feel awful."

"They're actually chasing scents." Jerry picked
a long stem of grass as he walked and pointed to
where the only indication of the dogs was the grass
heaving and flattening. "Miner loves hunting."

"What are they hunting?" Wiremu asked,
looking around. "There's nothing here."

"Rats," Jerry answered simply. "They're awful
pests, but Miner loves tracking them. That's how
he got his name. He has always loved digging deep
down in the burrows, and Dad once said he'd find
gold at that rate."

There was a moment's silence, then Taseu chuckled. "I get it! Goldmine . . . digging . . . a miner."

"It's funny how we give them names." Toni nodded. "Rima got hers because she was the fifth puppy in the litter."

"Tahi, rua, toru, wha, rima . . ." Wiremu chanted the numbers in Maori. "I reckon I'd like a dog called 'Toru.' It sounds strong."

The track leveled out near the top of a cliff. They could see the ocean below and hear the waves sweeping and crashing onto rocks that surrounded a wide, semi-circular bay with gray, rock walls that looked craggy and weather-beaten. The uppermost branches of an enormous Pohutukawa tree, brilliant with red flowers and dark green and silver foliage, were visible below the cliff edge, and they moved stiffly in the breeze as if they were suspended from the cliff. Jerry walked calmly forward toward the edge of the grass.

"Wait here." He held up a hand for them to stop behind him. "I'll just check to see if it's safe. It gets a bit slippery around the tree roots sometimes."

They waited while he walked forward, then suddenly his foot slipped out from under him and he disappeared over the edge with a bloodcurdling yell.

"He's gone over!" Wiremu began to run forward, but Erana grabbed him.

"Don't be stupid!" She kept a tight grip on his shirt with her hand. "You could go too!"

Toni's heart was beating fast as she walked forward cautiously. She had to see what had happened to Jerry. Just near the edge where the long grass flattened out, she lay down on her stomach and inched forward. She could hear somebody doing the same thing behind her, but she only had eyes for what lay in front. Her stomach churned as she had fleeting visions of Jerry lying on the rocks below or dangling from the cliff.

"Just kidding!" Jerry's head popped up directly in front of her, and she screamed loudly a second before Wiremu yelled.

"What the—!" Wiremu gripped some chunks of the grass stems and wrenched them out with his hands. "What do you think you're doing, Jerry? You scared us!"

Toni sat back in the grass with her hand to her heart, feeling it racing fast.

"That really wasn't funny, Jerry." She tried to keep her voice from shaking. "I thought you were dead or something."

"Sorry." Jerry really did look apologetic as he watched her face. "It's just such a good trick. It's like a tradition when new people come over."

"Then it's no wonder you don't have many visitors," Wiremu muttered and frowned. Then his curiosity got the better of him as he realized that only half of Jerry was actually showing. "So what's down there?"

Once they realized it was safe, Erana and Taseu were right behind Toni and Wiremu as they walked toward the edge. Still cautious, they leaned over as Jerry stepped back and waved his arms out wide.

"Welcome to the 'Cliff Hanger'—my home away from home."

Just below the edge of the bank, he stood on a solid platform of soil and leaves formed by the heavy roots and trunk of the Pohutukawa tree. The gnarled branches, beaten and twisted from years of battering by sea and wind, created a natural canopy of leaves and flowers. Large flax bushes growing down the cliff at the sides of the tree among more twisted roots formed a precarious but natural pathway down to the beach.

"This is great!" Taseu slid over the bank to stand beside Jerry. "This is awesome!"

Toni was more cautious as she lowered herself onto the flattened surface. As she turned, she gasped at the sight of a cavelike area cut out of the bank, forming even more of a shelter. At the back there was a small wooden crate and a blanket.

"Do you really stay here?" she asked Jerry.

"Not at night . . . just in case I sleepwalk." Jerry grinned. "But I like to come up here and watch the bay. If I can't get over to school I sometimes come up here and do my work."

"School?" Erana joined them, slithering down the long strands of grass. "Where do you go to school?"

"Over on the big island." Jerry pointed behind them. "I go by boat, but sometimes the wind is too bad and the water is really rough, so I have to work at home."

"Man!" Taseu shook his head. "How good would it be to not go to school if it was too windy."

Erana didn't seem to hear him as she stared at Jerry. "You go by boat every day?"

Jerry nodded. "Mum or Dad take me on the boat, then I catch the school bus over to the other side of the big island."

"Wow!" Wiremu nodded thoughtfully. "I think I'd want to go to school if I got to do that. It'd be like an adventure every day of your life."

Toni watched Jerry's face as he looked thoughtful, then he nodded slowly.

"I guess it is. Life on the island is an adventure."

It was easy to lose track of time as they played among the huge tree roots and branches. The limbs were wide enough to lie down on, and the areas where the twisting roots worked their way into the cliff made natural rooms.

"I reckon this is as good as the coffin house." Wiremu lay along a tree branch with his hands clasped behind his head, staring at the sky. "I haven't seen a single spider."

"What's the coffin house?" Jerry sat on a branch below his cousin with his back leaning against the branch. "It sounds gruesome."

"It's our headquarters," Erana answered importantly, looking up from the necklace she was making with red flowers and silver Pohutukawa leaves. "We're the Coffin House Kids. We do service for people, and the coffin house is where we do all our planning."

"But why is it called a coffin house?" Jerry still looked puzzled.

"Because there are coffins stored there." Wiremu sat up. "It's an old cottage that belongs to Grandma, and she leases it to the funeral director to store the coffins, but we're allowed to use the attic for our headquarters. It's pretty cool—except for the spiders."

"We're still cleaning it up," Toni explained quietly. "But the spiders make their homes faster than we can clean."

Jerry nodded thoughtfully. "So what sort of service do you do?"

"Well, not much as yet." Toni smiled. "We sort of just got organized."

"Since we solved our first mystery." Wiremu leaned forward. "Our specialty is mysteries, but being of service is all part of the deal."

"Since we solved our only mystery," Erana corrected him.

"Well, you have to start somewhere." Wiremu grinned confidently at Jerry. "That's why we thought we could help solve this problem with the man that drowned."

Jerry frowned and shook his head. "I don't think you'd want to get involved in anything like that, and besides, it's none of our business."

"But what if we made it our business?" Wiremu was persistent.

"Wiremu, get the message! Jerry and Uncle Ammon have said it's not up to us, so stop going on about it." After bringing the conversation to an abrupt halt, Erana glanced up at the sky, where the sun was taking on a silvery hue. "What time do you think it is?"

The others glanced up, and Jerry shrugged. "It must be getting close to six o'clock."

"Six o'clock!" Taseu looked alarmed as he patted his stomach. "My tummy usually warns me it wants dinner around five o'clock. I haven't felt a thing."

Wiremu laughed. "It's all the sea air filling you up. You could get really skinny at this rate. Your mum won't recognize you when we get home."

Erana stood up straight away. "Should we be helping with dinner?"

"No." Jerry shook his head. "Dad said he'd fix it tonight. Fish and chips. Really fresh fish and chips. We caught the snapper this morning."

"In that case, we'd better hurry." Taseu was already climbing the tree roots up the bank.

Toni wasn't sure whether it was the sudden light that shone brightly from the bay area, but something made her turn around just before she followed him up. Through the dense foliage of the Pohutukawa she watched a boat move slowly into the inlet and maneuver over the deeper water offshore while keeping a safe distance from the rocky shelf that surrounded the bay. A man came out onto the bow of the boat and dropped an anchor overboard, then he stood up and removed the cap from his head.

"Hey!" Toni automatically dropped her voice to a whisper as if the man could hear. "Isn't that the dolphin man?"

"What? Why are you whispering?" Wiremu looked puzzled when Toni dropped to a crouching position. "What are you doing?"

She pointed silently toward the boat. "I'm sure that's the dolphin man down there. You know, from the ferry."

Erana took her time draping her new flower necklace around her neck before she turned to look, but then she leaned forward, squinting her eyes.

"I think you're right," she said, nodding. "I didn't see much of him, but that is the same color jacket he was wearing—it's quite an unusual beige—and he is quite tall. See how he has to bend under the cabin door."

"I can't see his face to know if it's him." Wiremu shook his head. "But that's the boat that was down in the channel earlier. I'd recognize all the fancy fishing things anywhere. He must be a pretty keen fisherman."

Toni was silent as she watched the man working around the boat, then she turned to Wiremu, a puzzled expression on her face.

"That's just it," she said, her brow furrowed. "Don't you remember? He said he wasn't interested in fishing." She looked at Jerry. "Why would somebody have such a fancy fishing boat if he wasn't going fishing?"

Jerry shrugged as he knelt beside her. "Maybe he's just having a holiday. There's nothing wrong with just going boating. Lots of people do that out here."

"No." Toni nodded thoughtfully as she slowly stood up. "No, I guess there doesn't have to be anything strange about that."

Wiremu stopped as he heard the hesitant tone of her voice, and he watched her face closely as she took another long look at the boat.

"What's the matter, Toni? Are you worried about something?" He stepped back to stand beside her.

"Not exactly worried." Toni shook her head slowly. "I don't even know what I'm thinking, really. It's just a feeling I had on the ferry when we were talking to him."

"A bad feeling?" Jerry asked quietly while he too watched the expression on her face.

"Not exactly 'bad.'" Toni hesitated, and then her cheeks colored slightly. "There's just something that feels . . . odd, somehow." She stood up straight and gave a short laugh. "But I'm probably just being too suspicious. I've been listening to all Wiremu's talk about solving mysteries, and now I'm even starting to create them in my mind."

Wiremu chuckled. "Well, at least we'll be ready if one ever does happen."

"Oh, my goodness, what's he doing now?" Erana spoke suddenly, resting her elbow against the branch and watching the boat intently. "He just closed a black plastic bag with something heavy in it and dropped it over the side of the boat."

"He might just be cooling some food or something." Wiremu knelt back down beside her.

"Mmm . . . could be." Erana wrinkled her nose. "But before he dropped it over he looked up and down the bay—like he was scared someone might be watching him."

They were all silent as they watched the man brush his hands on his trousers, glance quickly around the bay again, then swing himself down below the cabin deck.

"You know, I reckon he might be up to something." Wiremu barely breathed the words. "And I'd really like to know what is in that plastic bag."

"Not that you're going to find out." Jerry looked quickly at his cousin. "That'd be asking for trouble."

Erana rolled her eyes again. "But that's what Wiremu is best at," she told Jerry. "So you'd better get used to it."

CHAPTER FIVE

"Erana." Toni prodded her friend's shoulder gently. "Erana, are you coming fishing?"

"Wha—" Erana mumbled as she turned her head on the pillow and settled back into its softness.

"Are you coming fishing?" Toni poked her again, a little bit harder this time. She knew from having lots of sleepovers with her that Erana didn't like getting up in the morning. "We're going out to catch breakfast."

"Breakfast?" One sleepy eyelid lifted. "Why can't we just have cereal?"

"Because we're on an island." Toni leaned back on her heels. "It's part of the adventure."

"I'm not adventurous," Erana mumbled into her pillow. "I'm fine with cereal. Wake me when you get back."

"No, you've got to come." Toni was persistent. "We can watch the sunrise while we're fishing. It'll be fun."

A long, low groan sounded from the pillow, then the sheets moved slowly as Erana pulled her legs up until she was kneeling, but her face was still firmly pushed into the pillow.

"It better be really fun." She lifted her head to squint at Toni. "And it better be the best sunrise ever."

Toni chuckled as she watched her friend rub the sleep from her eyes. "I'll wait for you outside."

Rima was waiting out on the veranda when Toni opened the door, and she stood up expectantly, pushing her head hard against Toni's legs.

"Whoa. Don't knock me over." Toni repeated their morning ritual as she bent down and gave the dog a warm hug and received a lick on the chin in return. "So you still love me?" Another lick. "I love you too, Rima." Another lick. "And Jack does too."

"Is Erana coming?" Wiremu walked out from the house. "I had the hardest time waking Taseu up, and then he said his stomach still felt queasy from the boat trip."

"Or from the four pieces of fried fish and two plates of chips he ate last night." Toni giggled. "Erana didn't want to come, either, but I convinced her that she'd have fun."

Wiremu glanced up at the sky, which was beginning to take on a lighter, more silvery tone.

"Jerry says it'll be a good sunrise this morning." He frowned. "He was talking about which way the wind was blowing and how high the tide was and all sorts of things. I thought we just had to go out in the boat and catch the fish."

As he spoke, Jerry came around the corner of the house carrying two wooden oars and a bucket. Miner followed close by.

"Are you ready to go?" Jerry held up the bucket. "I've got the lines, and the bait's down on the wharf."

"We're just waiting for Erana." Wiremu pointed toward the cottage right as Erana walked out looking surprisingly fresh in a pink sweatshirt with her hair pulled back.

"I'm ready." She held up the small camera she'd received for her birthday a few weeks earlier. "Shall I take pictures?"

"As long as they're not of me." Jerry grinned. "That's forbidden."

They felt a cool breeze as soon as they walked onto the wharf, and Toni felt the hairs prickle on her arms and neck. Even the water lapping gently onto the rounded gray rocks on the beach looked cold and clear. She shivered and rubbed her arms. "My goodness, it's way colder down here. Should I bring a jacket?"

Jerry glanced at her long-sleeved T-shirt and shook his head. "You'll be fine once you get your life jacket on." He stopped beside a small tin shed and pointed to a row of bright orange buoyancy vests in various sizes hanging on pegs on the wall. "If you'll all find a vest that fits and grab one for me as well, I'll go and get the bait ready."

A few minutes later they filed onto the narrow wharf, and Toni instinctively rubbed her nose as the strong smell of fish wafted from a pile of containers. Behind the stack, Jerry was lowering a strange jellylike mass into the bucket.

"What is that?" Toni took a step back when she noticed rows of black-rimmed suction-type nodules along one side of a long, white, rubbery tube.

"Octopus tentacle." Jerry jiggled it in his hand. "Our bait."

"Oh." Toni gulped and took a deep breath as Wiremu bent down beside the bucket and poked the flesh with his finger.

"It's rubbery and squishy all at the same time." He held the tentacle up. "Imagine a really enormous one of these wrapping its tentacles around you and squeeeeezing." He bulged his eyes for effect while draping the tentacle close to his throat.

"You've been reading too many stories, Wiremu." Erana quickly took his picture while he posed.

"Not me." He chuckled and laid the tentacle back down. "I don't read. I just have a vivid imagination—or so Grandma says."

Soon they were all seated in a long, fiberglass dinghy. Miner and Rima sat close together on the jetty, whining quietly as they watched the children prepare to leave without them. Jerry primed a small outboard motor as he glanced out at the waves then up at the sky.

"There's not much wind right now, so we'll go out around the point." He nodded toward the front of the boat. "Can you slip that rope off please, Toni?"

He waited as she cautiously got her balance and then leaned forward to slip the rope over the wooden jetty post and throw it back into the front of the boat.

"So are we going to lift the craypots today?" Wiremu moved to make room for Toni to sit back down.

"Yep, we'll do that later this morning." Jerry gestured with his head toward a larger fishing boat anchored farther away from the wharf. "We'll be taking the big boat out." Jerry pulled on the starter cord, and the engine purred into life. "It may get a bit rougher later, but Dad knows exactly when to go out or not." Jerry ducked his head and added quietly, "He's a great sailor."

Toni glanced up at him. She could detect the pride in his voice. "Has he always been a fisherman?" she asked, shifting slightly on the narrow seat.

"Always . . . and his dad and my great-grand-father." Jerry nodded. "In fact, our ancestors were among the first Maoris to settle here, and they've always been fishermen."

"So do you want to be one too?" Toni was fascinated by Jerry's quiet confidence.

He nodded without speaking and steered the dinghy out toward the dark outline of a small, rocky island, maneuvering the boat so that it crossed the slight swell smoothly. Squinting, he looked up at the bright sky then out at the wide expanse of ocean, which was silvery and transparent in the morning light.

"I love everything about the sea," he responded simply.

They dropped anchor at the far end of a wide bay, well clear of the low-lying rocks at the base of the high cliff that towered above them. Jerry gave them each a handline and showed them how to bait the hooks with the pieces of octopus tentacle he cut up for them. They each cast their lines out, then watched as the weighted lines sunk down into the dark green water beneath them. Toni peered hard into the water.

"I can't figure out how it can look clear, and yet it's so dark that I can't see anything." She squinted, then opened her eyes wide as if it would help her see better.

"That's because there's nothing to see at the moment." Jerry pointed as the end of Wiremu's line suddenly jerked. "You can see things near the surface. Watch when Wiremu pulls the fish in."

"I've got a fish!" Wiremu yelled and began to stand, then quickly sat again when the boat swayed. "Whoa . . ." He pulled on the line as it strained and began to move across the water.

"Just start winding it in easy." Jerry gently pulled the line near the water as Wiremu began to wind it in. "You've got a pretty big one."

"Yes!" Wiremu's eyes widened as he caught sight of the fish coming up through the water toward them. "Here comes breakfast."

He pulled it over the side of the boat, where it lay still for a second. When he reached for it, it suddenly flipped itself vigorously several times so that it moved across the bottom of the dinghy. Toni couldn't stifle a little scream when the fish flopped near her feet, its rainbow-colored fin moving silently up and down.

"Oh, it's so pretty." She tentatively reached out a finger to touch the reddish skin dotted with bright turquoise spots, then she jumped again as the fish lurched. She held both hands back, clutching her own line. "But so springy."

Within an hour they had each caught one fish, and Erana had made them all pose with their catches so she could take photos. By the time Jerry started the motor again, the quiet hum of the engine was the only sound in the bay, and it seemed to echo off the cliff walls as he turned the boat in a wide arc, swinging out beyond the rocks. He pointed backward as the boat straightened.

"Back around there is that bay we saw the boat moored in last evening—where we played on the pohutukawa tree."

As he spoke, they first heard and then saw a large, white, inflatable dinghy powered by a big outboard motor come around the side of the cliff. At the sight of them, the driver seemed to hesitate. The engine faltered briefly, then the noise suddenly got louder as he revved the engine, taking the boat quickly out into the open water, where it seemed to bounce from wave to wave. It was over a hundred yards away, but Toni could see the man clearly.

"It's the dolphin man!" She pointed to the figure crouched over the engine, his head bent into the wind.

"Are you sure?" Jerry shaded his eyes as he watched the boat speed off around another small island to their left. "He's in a big hurry, whoever he is." He shook his head as he revved the engine of their own dinghy. "But he won't find anything much over there except our mussel farm, and he'd better stay well away from that."

"Do you think we should follow him?" Wiremu sat up straighter. "He might be up to no good."

"Whatever makes you think that?" Erana looked doubtful as she scrolled back through the photos on the digital camera. "Just because he's up at this crazy hour of the morning doesn't mean he's actually doing something wrong." She smiled as she held up the camera, its screen showing an enlarged picture of the man in his boat. "But at least I have pictures of him doing nothing or something."

Wiremu grabbed the camera and peered closely at the pictures, then he shrugged his shoulders. "I guess you're right. Maybe he just enjoys early mornings." He nodded and bent back down to inspect his fish in the bucket. "But it still wouldn't hurt to keep an eye on his boat while it's in the bay."

CHAPTER SIX

Erana decided to stay home with Auntie Mere while the others went with Uncle Ammon and Jerry to lift the crayfish pots. Toni was getting used to the fishy smell, but she still hesitated when she saw Jerry lift the lid off a large container of fish heads and bones.

"Eew." She tried not to frown. "Who ate them all?"

Uncle Ammon laughed. "We've just taken the flesh off and put it into the freezer. Now we'll use the remains as bait for the crayfish."

Within minutes of leaving the wharf, he directed the boat out toward the open sea. There were hardly any swells, and the water almost seemed like glass as they skimmed over it with barely a bounce. Toni lifted her face to the wind, and, closing her eyes, she let herself relax until she felt like she was floating, her body moving gently with the boat. The boys sat up at the front of the boat, and Jerry pointed out the rounded, colored buoys that bobbed in the water, marking the places where crayfish pots hung by long ropes.

When they neared the first fluorescent pink buoy, Uncle Ammon quickly turned the steering wheel and brought the boat to an abrupt stop beside the buoy.

"Ready, Jerry?" Uncle Ammon asked. "Let's show the boys how to work this." He cut the engine to a low hum, and the boat remained still while Jerry grasped a long pole with a curved metal hook.

Wiremu and Taseu stood behind Jerry as he reached over the side with the pole and swiftly caught up the buoy with the metal hook. It took just a few seconds to pull up the buoy and the attached rope and to wrap the rope around a metal winch that whirred on the wall beside him.

The children watched, fascinated, as the winch sucked up the rope and spit it out into a coiled pile on the floor.

"Any second," Uncle Ammon said, glancing over the side of the boat. "Yep, here it comes. Wiremu, you grab the side opposite from Jerry."

At the same time, Jerry and Wiremu leaned forward to grab the sides of a large, square, wire cage that suddenly appeared over the side of the boat. Inside, four large crayfish sat quietly, their heavy tails coiled back underneath their bodies, their long antennae trembling and waving through the bars of the cage.

"Wow, they're dark purple." Toni leaned closer to look, then jumped back in fright as two of the crayfish suddenly flapped their tails loudly and scudded around the cage.

"And really powerful." Wiremu had jumped too, but he tried to cover it up by watching the crayfish intently.

"Man, they're awesome!" Taseu was brave enough to actually poke his finger into the cage. "It's like they've got armor on. Look at all the spikes on their legs and backs."

Toni ventured closer again, intrigued by the bright orange spots decorating the crayfish's purple bodies. "So how many are we likely to catch today?" she wondered aloud.

"Oh, maybe three or four bins full." Jerry nodded his head toward a stack of plastic bins, then dropped a handful of fish remains into a basket in the top of the crayfish cage and sealed the lid. "Hopefully we'll fill all of those. This is a good part of the season, so that's why Dad needed extra help."

They repeated the process many times over the next few hours. Some of the pots were a long way out in the open sea, but others were really close to the rock cliffs of the many small islands. When they approached these, Uncle Ammon would negotiate the boat carefully, keeping it in reverse to go against the swell of the waves sweeping against the rocks.

"Isn't this dangerous to do when it's rough?" Toni stared up at the ragged cliffs then over at the rock shelf that extended out from beneath them. "Those rocks are so close."

Jerry nodded. "It can be." He was sitting beside her while Wiremu and Taseu took turns helping to pull the cage on board and Uncle Ammon controlled the winch. For the fourth time, the boys pulled an empty pot on board.

Wiremu shook his head. "Man, we're so close to the rocks and we're not even catching any. I thought this would be a good place."

"It usually is," Jerry said, frowning. "It does seem unusual that there's nothing in these pots."

Uncle Ammon nodded his head as he maneuvered the boat around to the next buoy. "I was just thinking the same thing myself." He pointed out to three buoys bobbing in a row. "If there aren't any crayfish in these pots, then I think we might have a problem."

"What sort of problem?" Toni asked, puzzled.

"Poaching," Uncle Ammon answered quietly. "A lot of casual fishermen who come out around the island are allowed to catch a few crays, but some take more than they're allowed."

"And sell them in town," Jerry added with a frown. "They look for our pots because they know we have bait down to attract the crayfish."

"Do they actually take them out of your pots?" Toni felt indignant.

Jerry nodded. "Sometimes. Or they go diving around the pots at night and catch the crayfish as they come up to the pots."

"That's really unfair." Taseu stood up with his hands balled into fists and poked a punch at an unseen target. "I wish I could stop them for you. I'd deal with them so they wouldn't want to poach again."

Uncle Ammon smiled at his enthusiasm. "I must admit I feel the same way, Taseu. It's hard enough to earn a living out here without people stealing from you. That's why we started the mussel farm, but we've even had trouble with that lately."

"What?" Wiremu frowned. "Do people poach them too?"

"If they can." Uncle Ammon nodded again. "But the farms are closer to shore, and the locals know our boats, so they tell us if they see anybody else near." He revved the engine again. "But poachers usually hit at nighttime or early morning—when people can't see them."

Toni felt Wiremu's look even before she saw it, and she knew they were both thinking the same thing. The dolphin man had been heading for the mussel farm very early that morning. What other reason could he possibly have for going near it?

Even as they were thinking it, Jerry turned to his father. "I forgot to tell you, Dad. We saw a guy heading toward the farm early this morning. He was in a big, white inflatable, and he went pretty fast when he saw us."

"We even know who he is," Wiremu broke in. "He was on the ferry with us, and he's sailing that big fishing boat that was out in the channel the other day."

Toni waited for a reaction from Uncle Ammon, but there was only the merest flicker in his eyes before he shook his head and revved the engine.

"He's probably just a nosy visitor," he said. He gave the engine plenty of throttle, and they all had to hold on tightly as the boat pulled out into the waves.

* * *

The water was so clear near the wharf that they could easily see the rocks and sand on the ocean floor.

"Just jump." Wiremu stood close behind Erana as she clasped both arms around her body. "It'll only be cold for a second."

She rolled her eyes at him and shivered. "That's what you always say. I don't have as much covering as you. I freeze longer."

"Just swim harder." Wiremu repeated his usual instructions. It seemed like he had to coax Erana into the water every time they went swimming. "Then you'll get warmer quicker."

"I'm fine watching." She shook her head, then walked back along the wharf. "I'll go in from the beach."

The wharf extended from the bank out into the deeper water, but to the side of it, the shoreline curved around to form a small, natural bay. An assortment of body boards and kayaks provided plenty of material to play with, and the children headed for them as soon as they returned from fishing. Toni floated on her back in the water, her arms and legs spread out in a starfish shape, her eyes closed as she faced the sun's warmth.

"It's lovely, Erana," she called out as her friend walked down to the water's edge. Toni had had no trouble getting into the water quickly because she loved swimming, but she understood Erana's reluctance. "Why don't you grab a body board and just float out?"

She opened her eyes and propelled herself forward in the water so that she could push the blue board toward Erana.

"Hey! Hey!"

Toni looked around quickly when she heard Taseu's excited voice from somewhere above her.

"Out in the channel. Look! Quick!"

She suddenly caught sight of him and Jerry up on a steep slope directly above the beach. They were standing up in the long grass and pointing out toward the sea.

"Dolphins!" Jerry yelled with both hands cupped to his mouth. "Lots of dolphins."

Then they were both running hard down the slope, leaping over the long grass with arms flailing to keep their balance. Taseu suddenly dropped and rolled, then popped up again and scrambled after Jerry.

"Quick!" Jerry burst onto the beach. "Get into the dinghy while I tell Dad!"

It only took a couple of minutes because Uncle Ammon had heard the yelling and was already running down to the wharf.

"We'll take the big boat," Uncle Ammon quickly directed as the children swam and ran to the boats. "We should make it."

Toni could almost feel her breath stopping as they moved the boat out into the channel to where the silvery-gray shapes were just visible. As the hum of the boat's engine throbbed through the water, it seemed to act like a magnet, and within seconds they were surrounded by dolphins of all sizes, gently rolling and tumbling through the water.

Ammon cut the engine and watched the group carefully for a minute, then said, "It doesn't look like there are any babies. You can go in."

"Go in?" Wiremu's voice was barely a squeak, and he coughed loudly. "In with them?"

"In the water?" Taseu's eyes were wide. "Swim with them?"

"You won't get the chance often." Jerry was already lowering himself out of the dinghy. "Just don't make big splashes or too much noise."

Toni watched as he sank into the water and dog-paddled to keep himself afloat while he looked around for the dolphins. She saw one surface behind him, and her breath caught in her throat as it eased forward and Jerry was lifted by the swell of water.

"Are you going in?" Erana was already pulling her camera out of its case. "I'll get some pictures."

"Are *you* going in?" Toni's voice quivered slightly with excitement. She wanted to so much, but she also felt scared.

Erana shrugged her shoulders and pulled a face. "I might, but I'd rather get the pictures. Go on . . . I dare you."

Almost as if the dare was all she needed, Toni turned and slid off the side of the boat, dropping into the channel water that was several degrees colder than the water near the wharf. She sucked in a deep breath and tried to calm herself as she watched a large gray dolphin surface about five feet in front of her. She could see its head just beneath the surface, and dark, friendly eyes seemed to be watching her.

"It's coming," she heard Erana whisper above her as the mammal eased itself through the water until she knew she could reach out and touch it.

"Oh, my." She couldn't resist reaching out a hand as the huge body surged beside her. For a second she felt the slippery coarseness of its skin, like wet sandpaper. In places there were deep scars, as if it had been attacked, and she wanted to touch them, but at the same time she didn't want to. Then it suddenly dropped beneath her. Not being able to see it was even more scary, and she felt her stomach churn.

"Whoa." Taseu let out a stifled yell, and Toni turned quickly and watched as he seemed to lift out of the water. A smaller dolphin rolled by him, grinning lazily, then disappeared. "This is so, soo cool."

His teeth were chattering, but Toni knew it wasn't from the cold. There was something mysteriously calming about being in the water with these creatures, and yet it was almost terrifying at the same time.

They stayed in the water for nearly ten minutes. Uncle Ammon tied two ropes to the back of the boat, and they held on while he towed them along behind the boat in a wide circle. The dolphins seemed to understand that they were playing and swam along with them, keeping their distance most of the time but occasionally venturing in among them.

Then it was as if an unseen coach blew a whistle to end the game. With one accord, all the dolphins moved away to one side. Then the water swelled as they lifted and dived, and they were gone.

Toni quickly rotated as she treaded water, hoping for a final glimpse, but the water was lapping smoothly around her. She glanced over at Wiremu and Jerry, who were watching the water as well.

"I think I could have played with them forever," Toni exclaimed, swallowing hard and straining her eyes into the distance. "That was so amazing."

Jerry was treading water beside her. "You were lucky," he said. "I've only been able to do that a few times before."

"Man, I can't wait to tell them about this at school," Taseu spluttered as he swam over beside them and bobbed up and down. "I'm sure that small one wanted to be my friend. He kept swimming right up beside me."

"Do you think you could train them?" Toni asked the question almost longingly. "Like in 'SeaWorld,' but keep them in the open." She swam slowly to the back of the boat and waited for the others to climb up the ladder.

Wiremu pulled himself up the ladder then turned to hold a hand out to Toni. "Like that program I saw on TV where they trained the wild dolphins to come and be friends with disabled kids. It was so cool." He reached down to give Jerry a hand too. "I reckon you should find one to be your pet, Jerry, then we could come and play with it."

Uncle Ammon looked at the four shivering children now standing on the deck of the boat and laughed. "I think it might be a little bit hard to pick up a spare, friendly dolphin—even on Great Barrier." He started the engine and headed the boat back to the jetty. "But then again, if you were going to find one, this would definitely be the best place to look."

CHAPTER SEVEN

"I'm so glad the dolphin man told us about the dolphins before we swam with them." Toni finished wiping a plate with a cloth and set it on top of a pile on the bench. "I was thinking of all the things he'd said as I watched them. It made them more real somehow—like I understood them."

"It was like that, wasn't it?" Wiremu cupped some soap bubbles in his hand and rested them on top of a glass. He was supposed to be washing the dishes but was more preoccupied with his bubble sculptures. "I guess that's why the teachers make you study things before you go on school fieldtrips."

"Well at least you've figured that out, Wiremu." Erana set more dishes on the bench for him to wash. "Grandma's been trying to tell you that for years—if you study you'll actually learn things!"

Toni nodded as she reached absently for another plate. "I keep thinking about how much that man knew." She hesitated. "And I've been thinking . . . I want to be like that."

"Like the man?" Wiremu was half listening.

"Not exactly like him." She searched for the right words. "I mean, I want to study more about animals—really study. Like a career." She stopped, almost embarrassed to say it out loud.

"Do you mean all animals or just sea animals?" Jerry leaned against the bench and joined in the conversation. Toni quickly looked up to see if he was laughing, but she could only see genuine interest in his eyes.

"Um, I've always said that I wanted to be a marine biologist, but this time . . . I think I'm really serious," she finished quickly.

Jerry nodded his understanding. "Well then, you should start finding out more about it. Dad has a friend from university who's now working over in Florida in a marine research program. She works with dolphins and does everything she enjoys all day long."

Toni's eyes widened. "All day long? That would be so awesome."

Wiremu's eyes lit up. His soap sculptures were drying up, so he had finally started paying attention. "Do you mean I could do sports all day long if I wanted?" he wanted to know. "Man, then it would be worth going to school. Hey Taseu, I know how you can get to play with engines the whole time."

"Leave school?" Taseu's face brightened.

"No, you just do whatever you want at school." Wiremu grinned broadly until Erana interrupted.

"No, you don't." She pretended to punch his arm. "And you know it." She held up the fingers on one hand and pressed each finger in turn. "You think about what you would like to be when you grow up. You find out all the best subjects to take in high school, and then you study at university or in a course until you're qualified to do what you want."

"That makes sense." Taseu held out both hands as if he'd already made the decision. "I'll go to university and then I'll build super-engines. Are there any more of those pancakes left?"

They all laughed as he searched the kitchen bench, but Toni just kept wiping the plate thoughtfully. She really did want to spend her time with animals, but she'd never thought of it as a job.

Wiremu watched the expression on her face. "Has that given you something to think about? You're looking all thoughtful."

"Mmm." Toni nodded shyly. For all his joking around, Wiremu often seemed to be able to guess what she was thinking even before she realized it. "I never thought that I could actually do that."

She smiled. "Now I can't wait to see Dad and talk to him about it."

There was another brief silence as Wiremu ran his finger along the edge of the bench. Then he took a deep breath. "You know you might have to talk to Sandy about it too."

Toni froze, then glanced up at him. She could see the questioning look in Wiremu's eyes as if he were testing her reaction. Slowly, she nodded. "I guess . . ." She swallowed hard and smiled. "I guess that's okay with me."

* * *

"So are we actually going to meet a pig?" Erana screwed up her nose yet again as she watched Uncle Ammon and Jerry make preparations for their day of hunting wild pigs. "Because I don't know that I really want to."

"Well, we may not have time to introduce you formally." Uncle Ammon chuckled at the expression on her face as he managed to loop a rope through Miner's collar with his good hand. "But you can be sure he won't be wanting to meet you."

Toni watched, then ran another rope around Rima's collar. Rima was already making whining noises in her throat as she strained to get into the boat beside Miner. The two dogs had become inseparable companions in the three days they'd been together.

"Calm down, Rima," Toni soothed. "We'll make you swim the channel at this rate."

"She'll get plenty tired after racing through thick bush." Jerry patted Rima's head, then took the lead and helped her jump into the boat. Her thick claws slipped and scraped on the bottom of the boat as she tried to get comfortable, and she finally sat down panting, her bottom on the low seat and her front paws on the floor.

"Rima thinks she's human." Taseu laughed and sat down beside her, and she responded by giving him a firm lick on the nose. "Pooh!" He waved his hand in front of her face. "I think she's been eating too much fish. That is seriously bad breath."

Uncle Ammon had promised to take them hunting as a reward for working hard at lifting the pots, although as Toni had listened to his enthusiastic descriptions of the intended hunt, she thought it was more a reward for him and Jerry. They obviously loved the idea of the hunt.

"Are we likely to catch a pig?" She didn't mind the sound of the hunt, but she found herself grimacing at the idea of actually catching an animal.

Uncle Ammon shrugged and started the engine. "It's probably too hot and dry. Pigs like to wallow and dig in mud where it's cool, so they may be hard to find while it's hot." He grinned. "But it's still a lot of fun trying."

They crossed the channel quickly, moored the big boat, and rowed ashore in groups in the dinghy. It was quite difficult leaping from the boat onto the piles of rounded gray rocks that formed the shoreline, but the dogs led the way, pulling hard on their rope leads so that the children had to follow quickly. Rima strained so hard to follow Jerry and Miner that she pulled Toni off balance on one of the large rocks.

"Rima! Just stop right now!" She spoke sharply, and Rima turned quickly at the unfamiliar tone. Toni had never spoken to her like that. "Now slow down and behave yourself!" Rima's head drooped to one side, and it only took a moment before Toni was on her knees with her arms around the big dog's neck.

"I'm sorry, Rima, but you have to stay close," Toni murmured into the dog's neck. "I don't want you getting hurt."

"Or hurting you." Wiremu stopped on a rock beside them. "She had you moving pretty fast over those big rocks."

"She'll be fine now." Toni stood up and kept the lead close, and Rima obediently stayed close to her side. "I was more worried about her. I can't imagine what Jack would think if she got hurt."

A few minutes later they were all gathered in a small clearing in front of a forest of dense bush that extended back from the beach and up a steep hill. Miner was already sniffing the air.

"Does he know where he's going?" Taseu watched Miner lift his haunches and pull toward the bush.

"Not really." Jerry untied the rope, and in a second, Miner was off, disappearing into the bush and leaving only a few quivering branches to indicate where he'd gone.

"You always have a 'finder' dog. They run around picking up any scents, and then they chase the pig down. When they bark, we know they've found the pig, and then we let the other dogs go. They chase the pig and hold him till we get there."

"Then what happens?" Toni asked slowly, although she already felt she didn't want to hear the answer.

"Umm . . ." Jerry glanced up the hill and squinted. "We see how big it is—like the small crayfish," he answered evasively.

"You let it go?" Erana put her hands on her hips.

"Sometimes." He turned as his father came back into the clearing. "Are we ready?"

"Yep." Uncle Ammon pointed to their left. "I think we'll be heading upstream and then up the hill." He glanced at his watch. "We won't let him go too long or we might just be letting ourselves in for a long, hot walk. Miner will keep going all day if we let him."

It was still a long, hot walk, and sometimes it felt as if they were traveling almost vertically. They eventually kept to a narrow path that wound its way along a sharp ridge then plunged back into the bush. It was pleasant walking through the native trees and shrubs—their brilliant green leaves of different tones and shapes provided a natural filter to the sunlight that streamed down from above them.

They could hear the faintest whisper of the ocean waves somewhere below them, but the main sounds were the whistling and warbling of birds and the crunching of their own footsteps. Erana and Toni lagged behind the others, distracted by their discoveries of tiny bush mushrooms, strangely shaped stones, and intricate spiderwebs. Uncle Ammon and Jerry walked on ahead, tracing the trail until they both stopped on a bank just above the children's heads.

"Look back there, kids!" Uncle Ammon pointed back behind them. "What can you see?"

They all stopped and obediently looked back at the mass of bush and trees.

"Umm . . . what are we supposed to see?" Wiremu voiced all of their thoughts.

"Look at the shape of the ground," Uncle Ammon said, walking back toward them. The children all stared at the ground under their feet, and Uncle Ammon laughed. "Not right at the ground." He spread his arm wide. "Can you see how the ground is all terraced in levels?"

Toni followed the sweep of his arm with her eyes, and suddenly she began to see the shape of long steps cut along the hillside. She could make out two levels up above them and several below until the bush obscured them.

"There are levels," Erana said, turning in a full circle. "They go both ways right along the side of the hill." She turned again. "Who did it?"

"Your ancestors," Uncle Ammon explained, sitting down on the terrace level behind him. "This is an old Maori *pa*—a fortress against being attacked." He pointed in the direction of the sea and the island where he lived. "When they were being attacked by other tribes, they'd leave the island and come up here for protection. They built these terraces and put sharp wooden posts on top of them." He bent down and picked up a smooth gray rock lying covered by the decaying leaves on the ground. "They would bring up rocks from the beach as missiles to throw down on the enemy."

"Man, that would have been amazing!" Wiremu pulled himself up onto the level above and made a throwing action. "Just like David and Goliath."

"What about Captain Moroni?" Erana pointed to the terraces. "Remember in the Book of Mormon, how he got all his troops to build terraces of earth around their city, then he put timbers on top of the terraces and spikes on top of the timbers—"

"And they built lookout towers and threw down stones!" Taseu broke in, remembering the story. "It would have been just like this."

"My dad showed me that part. It says that Moroni built them in a way the children of Lehi hadn't even heard about when they were in Jerusalem," Toni said, nodding. "Now I see what he meant."

"But we're descended from those people in America, eh?" Wiremu held out his arm and lightly pinched the dark brown skin. "From the Lamanites."

Uncle Ammon nodded thoughtfully. "The people of the isles of the sea. If I remember right, Captain Moroni was a pretty good leader."

"Yeah, like he was a strong and mighty man with perfect understanding," Wiremu quoted, flexing his bicep. "I really like that part 'cause I reckon I'd be like him."

Uncle Ammon hesitated and glanced at his son. Then he said, "I remember my mother telling me that Captain Moroni was a man very much like Ammon. That's why she gave me my name."

Jerry looked up quickly, and Toni watched in surprise as the color slowly rose up Uncle Ammon's neck and cheeks. He stared at the ground for a second, then stood up abruptly and said, "But he obviously wasn't talking about this Ammon, was he?" Then he swung down off the terrace and walked away up the trail.

Jerry took a deep breath and shook his head as he watched his father leave. No one else spoke until Toni walked over to Jerry.

"Is . . . is everything okay?" she asked quietly.

"Sure." Jerry shrugged. "My dad knows the scriptures pretty well but he just hasn't been to church in a long, long time."

"Oh." Toni cleared her throat. "But he is a really great man. Anyone can see that."

"My dad's the best." Jerry almost smiled, then he lowered his head. "I just wish he wanted to be at church with Mum and me. I don't think he really thinks about forever."

They kept walking, and soon they had forgotten the awkward moment, focusing instead on the entertainment Wiremu and Taseu provided. The two energetic boys used the terraces to take on the roles of Samuel the Lamanite preaching from the walls and Captain Moroni rallying his people with the Title of Liberty.

"In memory of our—Aaah!" Taseu bellowed as he suddenly ducked with his arms over his head while Wiremu dived to the ground and rolled to the side of the path.

"What was that?" Both boys yelled, their eyes darting from side to side, trying to locate whatever had just attacked them. Then they saw Jerry leaning against a tall tree laughing soundlessly with his hand holding his stomach.

"What's so funny, Jerry? What was that?" Wiremu demanded.

Jerry snorted, trying hard to change his laugh to a grin, and pointed to a tree farther up the path. A very large bird sat stolidly on a slender branch, its weight making the branch bend dangerously. It chortled at them and turned its head almost completely sideways.

Jerry finally gasped and shook his head. "*Kereru*. A wood pigeon. They fly low when they're full."

"Full of what? Lead weights?" Wiremu frowned as he stood up. "It nearly took our heads off!"

"It sounded like a helicopter landing." Taseu folded his arms and frowned at the seemingly fearless bird. "Right on top of us."

Jerry coughed and pointed back down the trail. "They get a bit dozy when they eat certain types of berries." He chuckled. "By the looks of him, that one must have eaten a truckload."

Toni watched, fascinated, as the kereru made a supreme effort, beating its broad wings loudly to lift itself off the branch and fly off to another bush. "Do you—"

"Shush, everybody!" The children froze as Uncle Ammon's voice filtered down to them in a muted whisper. "Listen."

They all stood still and silent, straining to hear anything among the bush noises. At first there didn't seem to be anything, but then they all heard Miner barking somewhere below them. Jerry pointed down the hill and turned to his father. Uncle Ammon nodded and gestured to Toni. "Let Rima go so we can follow her."

It was as if Rima recognized that her moment had come. She stood up, the short hair on the back of her neck bristling as Tony took the rope off of her collar.

Jerry bent down and whispered in her ear. "Find Miner, girl. Go find Miner."

Then she was gone, racing into the bush without hesitating, closely followed by all three boys and Uncle Ammon. Toni and Erana looked at each other and turned to follow, but the bush had already closed around the running bodies. For a few minutes they pushed their way through the tangles of branches and foliage, then Toni stopped.

"You know what?" she asked, staring into the bush.

"We could get lost really easily?" Erana touched a branch beside her. "All these trees look the same to me."

Toni nodded. "I think we were supposed to keep up."

"But we didn't." Erana shrugged nonchalantly, but Toni could hear the doubt in her voice. "What do you think we should do?"

"Ummm . . ." Toni glanced around. "We haven't come too far. I think we should go straight back where we came from and wait for them to come back."

Erana took a deep breath and looked down the hill. "They probably won't like coming back up the hill."

"They probably wouldn't want to be searching for us all over the place either." Toni turned round and began walking back. "My dad always says to stay put if I get lost, so we'll go back to where they left us."

Toni had to admit that even that was easier said than done. The two girls had to keep ducking their heads to avoid branches, and to make things worse, the ground looked the same everywhere.

After they had trudged through the bush for several minutes, Toni stopped and looked around. "I think we should have gotten back by now. I can't even see the terraces."

"So now what?" Erana dropped her hands down to her sides.

Toni looked up the hill and made a quick decision. "We'll go straight up. There's blue sky just up there through the trees, so we must be near the top. We'll wait up there."

They were actually very close to the ridge that ran along the top of the hill, and within minutes they stood looking out over a magnificent view of the channel dotted with islands.

"Oh, wow," Erana breathed, shading her eyes with her hand. "This is so cool. Look how blue the water is."

Toni nodded, then she pointed down to the right. "Look there, just around the point. That must be Uncle Ammon's mussel farm," she said, pointing at the orange and black dots that were actually large plastic buoys. Then she pointed toward some even tinier, colored dots bobbing near the rocks of a nearby island. "And those must be the markers for the crayfish pots. It's so weird to be able to see them so clearly all at once—like a big movie screen."

They sat down to wait and silently enjoy the view. A moment later Erana suddenly sat up and squinted into the sun. "Hey, there's a boat going over to those markers."

Toni followed Erana's gaze down to the water, where a white inflatable dinghy with one person in it was pulling in close to a buoy from the direction of the mussel farm. The girls watched as the driver cut the engine and dropped something over the side. Then he put something on his head.

Erana copied his movements with her hands. "He's going diving," she exclaimed. "He put a snorkel and mask on, and see . . . he's got one of those oxygen tanks."

As they watched, the man flipped over the edge of the boat and disappeared into the water.

"But why is he diving near the pot?" Erana wondered with a worried look on her face. "Do you think he's trying to steal out of it?"

Toni shook her head slowly. "I'm not sure, but if he's wearing an oxygen tank, he must be planning to stay down there for a while." She glanced up at the bright blue sky. "It's not exactly early morning or nighttime, which is when Uncle Ammon said poachers usually strike."

"So what could he be doing?" Erana twisted a curl of her hair in her hand as she stared down at the water.

Toni took a while to answer because a movement near the inflatable boat caught her eye. She leaned forward and shaded her eyes against the sun. "I don't know, but can you see down there . . . to the right of the boat?" She gasped. "I think it's a shark! It's circling around the boat."

"What!" Erana peered closer and held her breath. "Oh, my goodness. I think it is." Her eyes grew wide. "It might get the man!"

They watched helplessly as the dark fin moved slowly around the boat, occasionally disappearing then resurfacing. Each time it went under the water, the girls held their breath.

"If he comes up to the surface, it's bound to get him." Erana whispered, almost afraid to breathe.

"But what if it gets him under the water?" Toni put a hand to her throat. Any thoughts about what

the man might be doing near the pots were suddenly overtaken by fear for his safety and a feeling
of total helplessness. Were they going to be wit-
nesses to a shark attack? There was nothing they
could do from this distance.

"Oh, my goodness. He's come up—Look!"
Erana pointed to where the man had surfaced several meters from the boat. "But look at the
shark—it's circling around the back. He won't be
able to see it! Oh, my goodness!"

Toni held her breath as the fin slid through the
water toward the man. He wasn't moving. Had he
seen it yet? She closed her eyes and looked away.

"It's right there—He's . . ." Erana's shrill voice
turned to a gasp. "He's cuddling it!"

"What!" Toni's eyes flew open, and her fists
clenched the grass beneath her hands as she stared
at the scene far below them. "He really is." Her
voice was barely a whisper. "He's playing with it."

They watched as the man held onto the omi-
nous dark fin and was pulled through the water
until he let go. Seconds later the dark shape broke
the surface of the water and soared in a graceful arc
over the man's head.

"It's not a shark, it's a dolphin!" There was
relief in Erana's voice as she relaxed back onto her
knees. "He's playing with a dolphin."

"Thank goodness." Toni felt as if a balloon had deflated inside her chest, and she took a deep breath. "I was so sure he was going to be—"

"Well, he's not," Erana interrupted, suddenly serious again. She frowned at the man, who was now swimming back toward the boat with the dolphin. "But what are they doing now?"

The man climbed back into the boat briefly and threw something out to the dolphin. Then he flipped neatly back over the side, and both disappeared under the water.

Toni frowned and pursed her lips. "You know, I'm glad that wasn't a shark and the man is okay, but we should still tell Uncle Ammon about it. That guy shouldn't be near the pots!"

Erana nodded. "We might have to get the police in even if it's just to warn him to stay away." She smiled. "I'll bet Uncle Ammon will be glad we were able to catch him in the act. We might have saved him a whole heap of money!" Her eyes grew wide. "The boys are going to be surprised when we tell them about this! They'll be so sorry they missed it."

Toni was silent as she watched the still water below. Was that why the man had been so interested in Wiremu's exaggerated information about their holiday fishing project? Had he already been planning his attack on the pots? Maybe he'd even recognized Wiremu's description of their island. She shivered as she thought about their conversation. They might be the very reason he had come to their island!

Then in the distance she heard a crashing in the undergrowth and someone calling their names.

Toni turned to Erana. "You know what? I think we should tell Uncle Ammon before we tell the boys—just in case Wiremu gets any crazy ideas." Her brow furrowed. "I get the feeling there may be more to this than we think."

CHAPTER EIGHT

"I can't believe you girls got lost straight away," Wiremu said, chewing on the end of a long stalk of grass. "We went practically straight down the hill—you only had to follow us."

"Well, I can't believe you didn't wait for us," Erana shot back. She refused to let him make fun of them. "Gentlemen would have at least slowed down."

"We would have missed the pig." He shook his head at her lack of understanding.

"You didn't even catch the pig!" Erana exclaimed, speaking slowly and precisely to indicate it was him that was failing to understand her. "The pig ran away."

"But we saw it!" Taseu rolled over on his stomach where he was lying in the grass and rested his chin on his elbows. "It was enormous and nearly all black!"

They were all sitting on the top of the hill overlooking the houses and the bay. They'd finished doing chores at the house, and Uncle Ammon had announced that they didn't need to help lift pots because he had to go to Fitzroy to pick up engine parts. Jerry had decided to go with him, so the children had packed some lunch and gone for a long walk over the hills.

"Well, I think I'm glad you didn't catch it," Toni said, folding her arms on her knees. "I don't really like the idea of eating something you've just caught."

"We eat fish we've just caught," Wiremu countered. "And you buy meat at the butcher's."

"I know. It's just that I hate to think of animals dying." She hesitated. "Anyway, Erana and I need to talk to you about something else."

Erana leaned forward. "I'll say. You'll never guess what we saw yesterday—while you were lost."

"We weren't . . ." Wiremu started to object but stopped as Toni held up her hand.

"Anyway." She pressed her fingers together thoughtfully. "I think we really have a problem on the island."

"A problem with the stranger," Erana added importantly. "We saw him down at the pots."

"What stranger?" Taseu asked without looking up. He was more interested in a large insect climbing up a blade of grass.

"You mean the dolphin man?" Wiremu caught on straight away. "Where was he?"

Toni took a deep breath. "He was in the water, out by one of the small islands. While we were waiting at the top of the cliff, we had a really good view of the channel, and we saw him in his dinghy coming from the direction of the mussel farm. He went straight out to our crayfish pots and anchored near one and went diving."

Erana joined in. "But that wasn't all. While he was swimming we saw this shark circling around him. We were so sure it was going to attack him!"

She paused for effect, and Taseu finally sat up and paid attention.

"A shark? How big?" he demanded, holding up his hands as if to measure it. "Did it really attack?"

Wiremu was immediately skeptical. "It can't have attacked or you would have said something last night. Are you sure it was a shark?"

"Well, it turned out to be a dolphin." Toni began to explain.

"And he was playing with it!" Erana burst in. "And then they went diving together down to the pots!"

"Diving with a dolphin?" Taseu made a diving motion with his hand, then chuckled. "That's a whole lot better than a shark."

"But it doesn't change the fact that he was diving near the pots, does it?" Wiremu said, looking thoughtful. "With or without a dolphin."

Erana nodded. "We still think he might be stealing."

"Poaching." Wiremu corrected her without thinking, and then he frowned. "We need to tell Uncle Ammon."

"That's the funny part," Toni said, shaking her head. "I did tell him—last night while you guys were playing outside. We thought we should mention it to him first, but he hardly reacted at all. He just shrugged and said that lots of people go diving around the Barrier."

Wiremu raised his eyebrows. "So he wasn't worried? And yet he was the one who told us about the poaching and how much it's costing him."

They all sat quietly contemplating for a moment, then Wiremu stood up and said, "I reckon we should go and check him out."

"Who? The dolphin man?" Toni asked, surprised at his decision.

"Well, at least his boat." Wiremu motioned with his head in the direction of the bay on the other side of the island. "If he's poaching stuff, he's got to keep it somewhere."

"But we can't go on his boat!" Erana objected. "That's trespassing!"

"So is poaching," Wiremu argued, walking backward. "Who's coming?"

Taseu was on his feet in an instant, and Toni was right behind him. Erana sat for a while longer, then she slowly stood up and shrugged. "I guess someone sensible has to look after you."

They ended up running over the hill, and it only took a few minutes before they were all crouching among the limbs of the old Cliff Hanger. The white launch was still moored in the bay, and since the tide was at its lowest, the rocky shelf around the bay now extended closer to it.

"The dinghy's not there," Toni whispered, leaning out on the branch to check the far side of the boat.

Wiremu stared at her. "Why are you whispering again? Nobody can hear us from up here."

Taseu dropped his voice too. "Because it's more mysterious to whisper," he said, wiggling his eyebrows mysteriously. "And it helps to solve the mystery."

"You guys are crazy," Wiremu said, smiling in spite of himself. Then he lowered his voice and pointed down at the rocks. "I reckon we should go for a swim."

"I thought we were here to solve a mystery." Erana said, puzzled.

Wiremu looked at her in disbelief, then tapped his forehead. "Think about it," he explained gently. "We want to go for a swim—down there." He pointed again. "In the bay—where the boat just happens to be anchored."

"Oh." Erana frowned. "But I don't want to go for a swim."

Wiremu stared for a second, then smiled and patted the tree trunk. "Then why don't you stay up here and be the guard."

"For what?"

"For looking out in case the man comes back." Toni interrupted quickly. She could tell Wiremu's patience was running thin. "You watch out from here and yell if you see anything."

"Oh, okay." Erana smiled, but then she frowned again. "Are you going to swim out to the boat?"

Toni watched Wiremu take a deep breath, then nod as he began to climb down onto the level of branches below where they sat. As he climbed he tried to explain. "We're going to swim in the bay because the tide is nice and low and we can get *kinas* from off the rocks, but I'd better be careful because I've been getting cramps in my leg a lot lately."

"But you don't like kinas." Erana's protest fell on deaf ears as Toni and Taseu followed Wiremu down the steep leading to the bay. She sat back and folded her arms primly. "And you haven't been getting cramps."

"This looked a lot easier when Jerry climbed down," Taseu puffed as he reached out for a thick clump of flax leaves to slow his progress down the cliff.

"Jerry makes everything look easier." Toni balanced on a large root and looked around to see where to take the next step.

Wiremu was already several feet below them. He turned and indicated a flax clump to her right. "Go over there, then down to this one."

Toni looked at the path and back at Taseu, but he was now working his way down backward. When she looked down again, Wiremu was already nearing the beach.

"Okay . . . here goes." She chewed on her lip and took a deep breath before taking a long stride across to the bush, reaching out to grab the long strands of leathery flax. Her hand took hold, but her foot slipped down the side of the root base, and the next moment she was swinging over nothing.

"Help!" Her voice came in a wail as she tried to reach with the other hand, but there was nothing to hold onto. Both her legs swung and hit against the hard clay and rock, and she could feel the jagged pieces cut into her left leg. The pain made her cry out, and without thinking she released her hold on the flax.

For a second she felt nothing but a rush of air, and then her back hit another tree root.

"Toni!" Wiremu's voice came from far away. "Grab the root!"

In what seemed like slow motion, her arms instinctively closed around the nearest object, and then she was hanging and struggling to find firm ground with her feet.

"Toni!" His voice was nearer. "Don't move!"

Even with her breath knocked out she managed a weak laugh of relief when she felt her feet connect with another root and realized she wasn't falling any more. "I'm not going anywhere," she whispered against her arm as she tried to get her breath.

"Oh man! I thought you were a goner!" Wiremu's head appeared below her. "Are you okay?" She felt his hand on her foot checking to see if it was placed firmly on the root, and it was oddly reassuring.

"I'm fine." She gave a pitiful giggle. "I just thought I'd find a quicker way down."

"Trying to beat me again, eh?" Wiremu responded and patted her foot again. "You're actually pretty close to the bottom now." He held out his hand. "I'll give you a hand down."

Toni realized she'd had her eyes closed, and she opened them to see Wiremu's hand up near her elbow. She forced herself to lean forward and reach for his hand, then he maneuvered her to the next large rock and guided her over the other rocks that formed a natural staircase down to the beach.

"Good thing you stopped before the rocks." Wiremu had to clear his throat to get the whole sentence out. "You sure gave me a fright."

"I'm sorry," Toni whispered, suddenly realizing he was still holding her hand. He realized the same thing and instantly dropped it.

"I . . . um . . . I'm sorry too." He ran his hand through his hair. "I shouldn't have made you climb down."

"I wanted to climb down," she interrupted quickly and clasped both hands behind her back. "It wasn't your fault, honest."

There was a long silence, then Taseu dropped down backward onto the ground between them with a loud yell of triumph.

"Did it!" He raised both hands above his head and turned around. "Backward is the way to go! Wow, Toni—What happened to you?"

In a second both Toni and Wiremu realized that Taseu hadn't seen anything of her fall as he climbed down backward above her, and they both burst out laughing. Toni looked down at the long, deep scratches decorating her legs and lifted both elbows to check out the damages there. Her forearms and hands also had cuts, and small fragments of clay were clinging to the quickly drying blood.

"I guess I took the wrong track." She smiled weakly and brushed at the clay pieces. "I think I really do need that swim now."

The cuts stung badly as she lowered herself into the salt water, but she held her breath until the coldness soothed the stinging. She stayed crouching in the water until she almost couldn't feel anything.

"Does that feel better?" Wiremu walked up beside her, and his frown deepened as she held up one arm.

"Much better." Toni nodded and lowered her arm back under the water. "The salt water is really good for it." She stared at his shoulder. "Um, Wiremu . . . thanks for looking after me."

She couldn't look at him, and he found it difficult to look at her.

"Hey, what are friends for." He coughed. "But Toni—I think you're a real warrior."

She didn't know what to say, but she didn't have to say anything because Wiremu suddenly turned and dived under the water. It was several seconds before he surfaced some distance away and pointed out toward the boat. "I know it doesn't really seem important now," he called, "but shall we take a look at the boat?"

Toni hesitated, then she nodded. "I'm not so sure about going on board now. Can we just see it from a distance?"

She watched the grin spread across his face, then he disappeared under the water again with both arms flailing. He popped up as if in pain, grabbing a pale, wrinkly foot with both hands. "I think I feel a cramp coming on!"

He covered the short distance to the boat quickly, and even before Toni started swimming he was pulling himself up onto the bottom rung of a short stainless steel ladder at the back of the boat. He stopped near the top, and Toni saw him crane his neck forward to see into the boat's interior.

Her heart pounded crazily, and then she breathed deeply as he slid back down into the water and swam back to her.

"Nothing." He shook his head, and droplets of water spun out of his hair. "It's all just clean and tidy, and I couldn't see anything below the deck."

"I guess he wouldn't leave anything out for people to see." She began to swim for the shore. "But what do we do now?"

"I'm not sure." Wiremu lifted an arm to wave to Taseu, who was walking around the rocks to meet them. "Maybe we'd better ask Jerry. We might be getting in too deep."

Toni nodded. "Let's talk to him tonight when we go out night fishing." She stood up out of the water and shook herself. "I'm still confused about the dolphin man. He seemed quite nice on the ferry even though he asked you a lot of questions, but it's like he doesn't want to be seen now. And yet he's turning up in all these places that he shouldn't be—all the places you told him about."

"I didn't know he was using me to get information," Wiremu whined, immediately defensive. "He just seemed interested."

"But that's what I mean." Toni's skin prickled and she rubbed her arms. "Why was he so interested in anything you had to say?"

CHAPTER NINE

"Those are nasty grazes." Jerry made a face as he watched Toni apply ointment to the red scratches on her arms and legs. "How did it happen?"

"I just slipped down the bank," Toni said with a glance at Wiremu, who was sitting at the table watching her. "I missed my footing and went straight down."

Jerry shook his head as Toni handed the tube of ointment back to him. "Your father is going to wonder what we did to you."

"Oh, he's used to my having accidents." Toni pulled the three-quarter-length sleeves down on her T-shirt. "I've always been a bit clumsy."

"*Now* you tell me." Wiremu rested his chin in his hand. "I should have been asking for danger money for being your friend."

"That goes both ways," Toni retorted quickly, but she was smiling.

"Then I'm not too sure I want to take either of you out night fishing." Jerry sat down next to Wiremu at the table. "I could be asking for trouble."

Toni looked up quickly. "Oh, but you have to. I mean, I've really been looking forward to it."

Wiremu nodded. "It sounds a bit freaky, but I'm keen. What time do we go out?"

Jerry glanced up at the clock, then looked outside. It was after eight o'clock, but there was still a dim, silvery glow in the sky as the sun cast its last glowing rays across the water. All the trees and buildings were fast becoming featureless darkened silhouettes.

"Dad said sometime after nine would be dark enough, and we're lucky because there's hardly any wind tonight." He stretched his arms out in front. "Who feels like rowing the boat? It's better at night if we take the row boat."

"I'll row," Taseu answered immediately, although it appeared he was watching television from the couch. "I love rowing. My dad showed me how."

Wiremu and Toni looked at each other, and Wiremu lifted his shoulders. "I guess we'll find out."

* * *

"Wow, it's so dark, I can hardly see anything." Toni held her hand out in front of her as she sat down in the dinghy. "Funny how you don't notice it while you're sitting inside the house."

Taseu copied her and wriggled his fingers. "I wonder how the fish see where they're going."

Toni frowned and looked out at the glistening blackness lying in front of them. "You know, I've never thought about that," she admitted. "I wonder if they all go to sleep as well?"

Nobody responded. Once Jerry had untied the rope and pushed the dinghy away from the wharf, he pointed to the right, and Toni and Erana lifted the flashlights they were holding and shone the beams across the water in that direction.

"Okay, Taseu, out around the point over there," Jerry directed.

Taseu looked over his shoulder and peered into the darkness, gripping the oars in both hands, then he straightened. "I can't even see it," he complained. "Are we sure about this?"

"I'll direct you," Jerry said, settling down in the bow. "The tide is going our way, so it'll only take a few minutes."

It actually took a lot longer because they made a series of near circles across the small bay.

"My right arm is . . . a lot . . . stronger than my . . . left." Taseu grunted with effort as the left oar scudded across the surface yet again while the right oar dug deeply into the water. He then compensated by taking extra little strokes with his left to put the dinghy back on course. "I don't remember having this much trouble before."

He paused to flex his hand and suddenly realized that the others were laughing silently. "Okay, you all have a go at it if you think it's so funny," he said with a frown.

"No, no." Wiremu finally laughed out loud and had to hold his stomach. "We're enjoying watching. If only I could see your face."

Taseu began to giggle as well, and then the giggle turned into his famous deep, belly laugh, and the whole boat started rocking.

"Whoa, don't rock the boat," Jerry exclaimed, holding onto the side. "Do you want me to row for a bit, Taseu?"

Taseu wiped his eyes with the back of his hand. "Unless we plan to go fishing under the wharf," he said, trying to stop laughing, "I think you'd better. I'll practice a bit more tomorrow."

While Jerry rowed them out, keeping just out from the rocky shoreline, the other children had light-beam battles with the flashlight beams in the night sky. Within five minutes they were nearly around the point. Then Jerry paused, and the boat rocked gently in the darkness.

"Turn off the flashlights and see how black it is," he told them. His voice was low, and they quickly switched off the flashlights. "Now watch as I move the oar," he suggested.

They didn't notice anything at first, then Toni leaned forward. "There're lights! Lots and lots of teeny lights."

As if by magic, the water seemed to light up with the movement of the oar. A flurry of miniature lights would appear for a few seconds then disappear until the oar dipped again.

"What is it?" Erana whispered. "It's so beautiful."

"It's plankton." Jerry lifted the oar up and down more rapidly, and the lights flickered even faster. "Lots of little organisms in the water, and they're phosphorescent. When they get disturbed, they light up for a fraction of a second, so when there's heaps of them, they put on a real light show."

Taseu squinted his eyes to make the lights seem to run together. "There must be trillions of them to make that much light."

Jerry nodded. "Sometimes Dad and Mum and I go night snorkeling, and it's really awesome to swim through it. Mum says it's one of her favorite things. She calls it her personal fairyland." He stopped rowing again. "Wiremu," he directed, "get one of the handlines and drop it over the side. I've already baited it."

They waited as Wiremu pulled the line out of the bucket and then swung the bait and sinker gently on a length of line away from the boat. Instantly, the lights seem to fix themselves to the fine nylon as it traveled down through the water.

"Look at the bait!" Erana pointed. "It's like a light bulb."

They could see the path of the line clearly defined through the water by the lights, and they all watched silently.

"So do the fish light up when they swim through it?" Wiremu ran his hand through the water, and the ripples glowed on either side.

"I don't know about all fish." Jerry shrugged as he looked around at their position. "But Dad and I were coming home from dropping a load at Leigh late one night, and this dolphin came by us. I swear it looked like a meteor it was glowing so much. It was brilliant."

They had so much fun watching their lines light up in the water that it didn't matter that they only caught three small fish. And it wasn't until they had pulled in the lines and the anchor that Toni suddenly nudged Wiremu and bent her head to whisper quietly.

"The dolphin man," she whispered. "We forgot to tell Jerry about him."

"Tell me about what?" Jerry turned slightly, startling her.

"Um . . ." Toni looked quickly at Wiremu, and he nodded. "Um . . . well, you know the dolphin man . . . around in the bay."

Jerry didn't say anything, so she added, "The guy we saw in the dinghy going to the mussel farm?" When she finally saw Jerry nod in the darkness, she continued. "Well, Erana and I saw him from the *pa*. He was coming from the mussel farm again, and then he went diving by your cray pots."

"Right beside them," Erana emphasized. "And then this dolphin came up to him. Only we thought it was a shark and that it was going to attack him, and we didn't want to watch but we did, and then they were swimming together—the dolphin and the man."

"And we saw him dive again by the pots," Toni said to interrupt Erana's rambling flow of information. "But we never saw him come up again before you found us."

"So we went to check his boat this afternoon," Wiremu added, resting his elbows on his knees. "But I couldn't see anything."

"You went on his boat?" Jerry sounded really surprised. "You shouldn't do that."

"Uh . . . I was getting a cramp," Wiremu muttered. "And I only held onto the ladder for a bit . . . like I'm sure he would've let me if he was there."

"Gee, I don't know." Jerry frowned into the darkness. "I mean, he could have been poaching, but then people are allowed to get crayfish—just so long as they don't take more than their quota. It doesn't give you the right to go on board his boat."

Toni still didn't feel comfortable. "But why was he near your pots and your mussel farm?" she wondered aloud. "Why was he at the places that Wiremu mentioned when we met him on the boat?"

They all sat still as the boat rocked silently, then Wiremu suddenly clicked his fingers. "Hey! Do you realize that he's been at those places when he knew we wouldn't be there?"

"What?" Taseu looked confused.

"Think about it. He was out in the channel that first day and he would've seen all of us on the jetty but he didn't want us to see him. Then he anchors his boat on the other side of our island when there's a gazillion other islands he could've gone to."

"And he was out at the cray pots when we were over at the big island at the *pa*," Erana put in quickly.

Toni nodded thoughtfully. "And he was going to the mussel farm when we would normally have been asleep. But how does he know where we're going to be?"

Taseu shrugged his shoulders. "He could be watching us, just like we were watching him from the Cliff Hanger tree."

"That makes sense," Erana said, nodding, then she wrinkled up her nose. "No, it doesn't—why would he be watching us?"

"I don't know, but I feel like we should tell Dad what we're thinking." Jerry began to row again, pulling the oars deeply through the water as if the strain helped him think better. "He'll be really interested in this."

"But that's just it." Toni spoke quietly behind him. "I did tell him." She folded her arms to stop a sudden chill from running down her back. "And he didn't seem interested at all."

* * *

"Oh, no!" Toni wrapped her hand around her wrist and twisted on the bed to look at her bedside table. "I've lost my watch!"

"Are you sure?" Erana lowered the book she was reading onto her chest and lifted her head to check around the room. Then she lay back on the pillow. "Hang on, I remember you took it off when you got that fishing line caught on it. Where did you put it after that?"

Toni thought about everything she'd done since they returned from night fishing.

"I think I must have put it on top of that barrel thing at the far end of the wharf—the one near the bait container."

"Is it covered?" Erana asked.

"No, it isn't," Toni said as she stood up. "I'll have to go and get it. It'll get all wet if it's left out overnight."

Erana pushed herself up on her elbows. "You can't go down there in the dark. It's way scary."

"It'll only take a minute," Toni mumbled with her sweater already halfway over her head. "I'll take Rima and a flashlight."

"Are you sure?" Erana made to get up, but Toni shook her head.

"No worries. I'll go anywhere with Rima, and it's not like there's anything down there except dead fish anyway."

A few minutes later, Toni found herself tiptoeing as she made her way past the darkened house and down the narrow path to the wharf. She was glad for the comforting warmth of Rima's big body close to her leg while she shone the narrow flashlight beam around the stacks of large, plastic containers. They formed a low wall along the wharf where it angled out to the left, and they seemed even higher and darker in the pale circle of light shining down from a high pole. Toni made her way carefully around them to the far end, then knelt down to check the lid of the barrel where she thought she'd left the watch. Her fingers finally found the shape, and she gripped it tightly.

"Yes! Got it," she whispered to herself, and she set the flashlight down on its end on the top of another plastic barrel so that she could put her watch on. The light from the flashlight was almost obscured, and, as usual, the tiny catch on the metal band of her watch was difficult to fasten. She struggled in the dark, then, thinking she finally had the clasp secured, she pressed hard to clip it shut. The watch flipped off her wrist, and she heard it thud onto wooden wharf.

She quickly knelt down and felt with her hands along the damp boards. "Oh, I can't see it!" she whispered. Close beside her she felt Rima's body suddenly tense, and a low growl rumbled in the dog's throat as she turned her head toward the blackness offshore.

"What is it, girl?" Toni felt the words catch in her throat, and she strained to hear over the sudden loud beating of her pulse in her ears. "What can you hear?"

At first the only sound was the water lapping softly against the wooden posts of the wharf, then slowly she made out the regular slapping sound that she'd been listening to all evening.

Someone was rowing a boat toward the wharf!

She felt her stomach tighten, and she crouched even lower and wrapped her arm tightly around Rima's neck. If she stood up, the lights from the house behind her would make her clearly visible to whoever was approaching in the boat.

"Shh, girl. Quiet. We'll wait till they've gone."

She couldn't see past the containers, but she heard a faint rubbing sound as the boat made contact with the wharf. For what seemed like forever, Toni crouched, straining her ears, but there was no further movement.

After a few minutes she felt the muscle beginning to cramp in her calf, so she slowly eased her leg out to the side, keeping a careful eye on the direction of the boat. In the dark she didn't see one of the small containers they'd used for bait sitting on the edge of the jetty until she felt her foot knock against it.

"No!" she buried her face against Rima's neck to stop from crying out loud as the container splashed into the water below. Whoever was in the boat was sure to hear that! She waited for the sound of anything moving, but the first noise came from the other direction—from the house.

She listened to the definite rhythm of footsteps coming down the concrete path then echoing slightly on the wooden wharf.

Rima's body tensed even more when the murmur of voices drifted through the stillness, and Toni gripped her tighter.

"Any problems today?" The voice was muffled, but it was definitely a man's.

"No, it went well." There was the sound of a container being dragged. "I got to all the pots. I'm pretty sure nobody saw me. You did a good job keeping the kids out of the way."

Toni felt her breath catch in her throat. Summoning all her courage, she crawled to the end of the row of containers and leaned out. "Oh, Rima!" She nearly choked as her breath caught in her throat and her fingers tightened in Rima's fur. Even in the dim glow of the light post, she could still make out the figures standing by an inflatable dinghy. The dolphin man and—Uncle Ammon!

She struggled to think clearly and forced herself to listen to their conversation. "Not a good enough job, apparently." Something was being lowered into the boat. "Toni, the blonde one—told me they saw you near the pots from the hill."

There was silence, then Toni heard a muffled exclamation.

"Do you think they suspect anything?"

"I don't think so, but their curiosity might complicate things."

Toni barely breathed as she heard the sound of someone climbing into the boat. She strained to hear their last words.

"I don't want them involved. They were only supposed to be decoys."

"Don't worry, I'll handle them, but have you managed to get rid of Bob?"

The steady slapping of the oars against the water almost drowned out the dolphin man's last words, but they made the blood in Toni's veins run cold.

"No, but he won't be in the way for long. I've thought of a way to get rid of him—just like the other guy."

CHAPTER TEN

"Morning, Toni." Uncle Ammon interrupted his whistling to greet Toni as she walked into the kitchen with Erana. He sounded unusually cheerful, and he grinned broadly as he flipped a pancake and caught it neatly on the spatula. "I've got some good news for you this morning."

Toni didn't respond to his greeting. She had hardly slept at all during the night as the events down at the wharf had repeated themselves over and over in her mind. When she had drifted off a few times, it was only to wake not long after.

"Toni." Erana nudged her gently. "Did you hear? Uncle Ammon's got good news."

"I'm sorry." She attempted a smile but found it difficult to look directly at Uncle Ammon.

"Very good news." He carried a plate of pancakes out to the table. "Your dad called early this morning, and he and Sandy are coming out on the plane later today. We can pick him up about two o'clock at the Okiwi airport."

"Dad?" Toni shook her head. "He's not due until tomorrow on the ferry."

"I guess he must be missing you, then." Uncle Ammon smiled. "They're definitely coming today. I said I'd pick them up."

"They must be missing all of us." Taseu chuckled happily as he eyed the pile of steaming pancakes. "We can all go and meet them."

"Well, if everybody's coming, we'll need to leave right after lunch." Uncle Ammon produced a bottle of maple syrup. "I have some business to attend to at Fitzroy first."

Toni looked down at her plate, and suddenly she wasn't hungry. What sort of business did Uncle Ammon have that made him go out secretly and late at night with a stranger? She shivered slightly as she realized they weren't strangers at all—the two men obviously knew each other very well. So why had Uncle Ammon not even acknowledged knowing the dolphin man?

"Pancakes, Toni?" Erana's voice seemed to come from a long way off, and Toni forced herself to concentrate.

"Um, just one, thanks." She took one with her fork and laid it on her plate.

"Just one?" Uncle Ammon challenged her happily as he sat down. "And after I made them especially for you."

Toni felt her mouth go dry, and she swallowed hard. She had to tell the others about last night at the wharf. Her heart sank. What was Jerry going to say when she told him about his father?

* * *

The big pohutukawa tree seemed the logical place to go to talk about the new developments, so straight after breakfast and chores, Toni found a chance to whisper to Wiremu. "We really need to talk." She watched Uncle Ammon carefully as he cleared the table with one hand. He seemed to be in a really cheerful mood, and it frustrated her. "Something happened last night. Can we go to the Cliff Hanger?"

"Sure." Wiremu studied her face carefully. "What's happened?"

"I'll tell everyone once we're there." Toni took a deep breath. "But I'm not sure Jerry will want to hear it."

Half an hour later they settled themselves on the different branches and roots that they had adopted as their own. Wiremu and Jerry sat on the higher branches, Taseu and Erana lay back against some roots that had shaped themselves like armchairs, and Toni sat astride a large branch that looped back onto the bank. It moved gently as she sat on it.

Once they were all situated, Wiremu immediately took control. "So what happened that's got you so serious?" he asked Toni.

Toni felt the palms of her hands grow warm. She clasped them together, then glanced down at the white boat below them. The dinghy was still tied to the back of the boat.

"Well . . ." she started, chewing on her bottom lip. "Last night, before I went to bed, I discovered that my watch was missing."

"She'd left it down at the wharf," Erana interrupted immediately. "I saw her put it on the drum."

Toni waited, then nodded in agreement and continued. "I didn't want to leave it out in the night air in case it got wet, especially because Dad gave it to me for my last birthday."

"That makes sense." Wiremu was taking his role as group leader seriously. "Did you go down in the dark?"

"I took Rima down with me, and I had a flashlight." Toni rubbed her hands on her thighs. Telling the story now didn't make it anywhere near as scary as it had felt at the time. "I found the watch straight away, but then I turned the flashlight upside down on the drum while I put the watch on, but I dropped the watch."

"Did that catch go funny again?" Erana asked, remembering the trouble Toni had had before with the clasp.

"Uh-huh." Toni glanced at Jerry. He was lying back watching the leaves move above his head, probably wondering why they'd had to come to the tree to find out about her watch. "Anyway, I bent down to find it in the dark, and then I heard . . ." She deliberately paused for effect to see if Jerry would look up. He was still watching the leaves. "Then I heard someone rowing up to the wharf. And it was nearly eleven o'clock."

She saw his head come up then and felt a mixture of satisfaction and concern. How was he going to react to the next part?

"Then?" Wiremu was leaning forward on his branch, and even Taseu sat up.

"Well, Rima started growling, so I told her to be quiet, and then I heard the boat come up against the wharf. Then for ages, nothing happened, but I was too scared to move."

"Nothing happened?" Erana sounded disappointed. "At all?"

"No—I mean, yes." Toni waved her hand. "I mean, nothing happened for a while. Then when I thought my legs were going to break from crouching down, I heard footsteps on the wharf."

"Our wharf?" Taseu clenched his fists on his knees. "Who was it?"

Toni nodded and went on. "I couldn't see at first, and I wasn't going to come out to look in case they saw me, but then they started talking." She hesitated as even Jerry leaned closer. "Then I crawled out a bit, and I could just see them in the glow from that light on the pole."

"So who was it?" Wiremu was getting impatient.

Toni took a deep breath and glanced at Jerry. "It was Uncle Ammon . . . and the dolphin man."

"Dad?" Jerry screwed up his face in disbelief.

"The dolphin man?" Wiremu looked surprised. "I thought you were going to tell us it was thieves or something."

Toni wasn't sure what reaction she had expected, but it certainly wasn't the doubt that they were all showing. Even Erana had sat back and almost looked disappointed.

"But wait till you hear what they said!" Toni began to protest. "Uncle Ammon asked if there were any problems today, and the dolphin man said that everything went well, and that he got to all the pots today."

"All the pots?" Wiremu frowned. "Our pots?"

Toni shrugged. "I guess so, but listen. He said Uncle Ammon did a good job with us kids, keeping us out of the way, but then Uncle Ammon told him that Erana and I had seen him at the pots."

Taseu gave a low whistle. "You caught him in the act."

"Yes, but what act?" Erana asked, putting her head to one side. "We don't actually know what he was doing there."

Toni looked around at them all. "I'm not sure what he meant, but the dolphin man said he didn't want us involved—that we were only supposed to be decoys."

"Decoys?" Wiremu frowned. "Decoys for what?"

"I don't know, but . . ." Toni paused and shivered as she recalled the last part of the conversation. "The last thing I heard was Uncle Ammon asking if the dolphin man had gotten rid of somebody called Bob, and the dolphin man said that he wouldn't be in the way for long because he'd get rid of him just like the other guy."

"Oh . . . my . . . goodness." Erana barely breathed the words, but they seemed to say what everyone was thinking as they sat in silence, the only other sound coming from the whispering of the leaves in the breeze.

Finally Jerry sat up on his branch. "There's got to be a good explanation. My dad would never do anything bad!" He slammed his fist down on the branch. "Never! That guy's conning him into something!"

Toni watched his face flush a dull red color as he stared down at the white boat moored in the bay.

Erana shook her head. "But why would Uncle Ammon go out with the dolphin man late at night? Why would someone who's not interested in fishing be visiting a fisherman in the dark?"

There was a very long silence, then Wiremu blew a long, low whistle. "As bad as it seems, I think Toni is onto something."

"But what?" Taseu still looked confused. "Poaching? Isn't that what we thought the guy was up to?"

Jerry shook his head. "That doesn't make sense. Why would my father be poaching from someone else? He wants to stop others from poaching from him."

They sat in silence again, then Erana suddenly looked concerned. "It wouldn't have anything to do with . . . drugs and stuff, would it?" She put her hands to her cheeks. "I overheard Uncle Ammon talking on the phone to someone the other day. He said that because the Great Barrier is so far out, sometimes people use it for dropping off drugs."

Nobody spoke, then Wiremu folded his arms. "There's an awful lot of money to be made dealing in drugs." He glanced at Jerry, who had been sitting silently. "I saw it on television. Even just by the guys that make deliveries."

"My dad would never do that." Jerry spoke very quietly and stared at the ground in front of him, and Toni saw that his teeth were clenched. A small muscle pulsed in his jaw as he looked up, first at Wiremu, then around at all of them. "My dad may not come to church and he may yell at my mum and drink sometimes, but . . ." He took a deep breath. "He would never do anything like that. Ever."

Toni felt her stomach churn as he slowly stood up and pointed down at the boat in the bay. With determination in his eyes, he finally said, "I don't know why that guy is here, but I'm not going to sit here making up stories. I'm going to go and ask my dad what's going on."

Toni quickly got off her branch. "But what if it's something dangerous? Wouldn't he have told you or admitted to knowing the man?"

Jerry shrugged and lifted his head, then he looked straight at her. "Whatever it is, there's got to be a simple reason, or I've got to stop him from making a big mistake."

He started up the bank but stopped when Wiremu called out, "Jerry!" Wiremu got down off his seat and walked over to his cousin. "We probably

got a bit carried away, but we only want to help."
He glanced around at the others. "We won't say
anything, but if you need any support . . ."

Toni barely heard Jerry's response. "Thanks.
I'll let you know."

* * *

They were quite a subdued group as they gathered
on the boat before leaving for Port Fitzroy. Jerry had
announced that he would stay home and finish
some holiday homework assignments, and Taseu
had decided to stay with him. They both stood on
the wharf watching the others prepare to leave.

"I guess we'll only be a couple of hours," Uncle
Ammon said and looked at his son carefully, but
Jerry wouldn't meet his eyes. He turned away and
looked straight at Toni. In that instant she knew he
wasn't just going to do homework while they were
away. She swallowed hard and raised her hand.

"Take care." She kept her voice low, but she
knew he heard her because he made a half attempt
to smile and raised his head slightly in acknowl-
edgement.

"I will."

* * *

They made the journey into Fitzroy in about twenty minutes, and Toni found she was preoccupied the whole time with looking out for the white inflatable raft, especially as they rounded the point by the mussel farm. She felt her shoulders relax when there was nothing to be seen except the long rows of orange and black buoys.

Uncle Ammon pointed at some of the buoys that were almost submerged. "We'll get a good harvest this year," he said. "There's plenty of weight on those lines."

"Do people ever try to steal the mussels?" Wiremu pointed around the bay not looking directly at Ammon. "Or even tie other stuff to the lines?"

Toni watched Uncle Ammon hesitate and stare at Wiremu then turn the steering wheel and rev the engine.

"Sometimes, not often," he responded. He leaned back and pointed up toward the sky. "I think that'll be our guests coming in now."

A small plane was approaching and flew directly overhead before rising slightly over the bush-clad hills behind the harbor. Toni watched the wings tilt a bit erratically, then the plane leveled out and swung down out of sight.

"They're a few minutes early," Uncle Ammon said, checking his watch. "They'll have a bit of a wait."

Okiwi Airport was really only a long paddock with a tin shed at the end. When they arrived several minutes later, Erana was the first one out of the four-wheel-drive truck.

"There's no one here," she exclaimed looking around.

Wiremu got out behind her. "There's nothing here," he added. "Where's the plane?"

"Where's my dad?" Toni asked. She wriggled off the seat and held the door open while she looked around for her father.

Uncle Ammon closed his door and walked to the front of the truck before he answered her. "The plane had to leave almost straight away to fly over to Claris," he explained. "As for your dad, I'm not sure. He should be here."

Toni's shoulders slumped with disappointment as she looked around the deserted paddock.

"Hey, everybody!" Two tall figures appeared from inside the small shed. As usual, Professor Bradford was carrying his worn, brown leather briefcase bulging with papers in one hand. But his other hand was firmly holding Sandy Jenson's.

"Dad!" Toni ran the short distance between them and threw her arms around his waist. "We thought you'd missed the plane!"

"Hey, chickie!" Her father stopped and let Sandy's hand go to wrap his arms around Toni in a huge hug, lifting her off her feet. "We weren't sure how long we might have to wait, so the shed offered a bit of shade." He let her down gently, then looked over her shoulder at Sandy and the rest of the group. "We've been missing you all. It's been very quiet at home."

"Have you really?" Erana looked doubtful. "We've only been away for four days."

"Four days?" Professor Bradford smiled directly at Sandy. "It seems a whole lot longer than that."

"It seems like we've been here forever," Toni agreed. She glanced at Sandy, who was smiling back at Toni's father. They both looked very relaxed and happy, but at the same time a bit uncertain. Toni gave her father's arm a brief squeeze, then pushed him gently back toward Sandy. Professor Bradford turned slightly and stared at his daughter, then he took hold of Sandy's hand again and swung it gently. She laughed self-consciously, but Toni noticed that Sandy gave his hand a tight squeeze.

Toni felt her heart leap. Somehow it felt right seeing her father and Sandy together. It seemed like the last four days had made a big difference for all of them.

"They look really good together," Wiremu said quietly to Toni. Then he glanced at her and asked, "Are you okay with it?"

Toni hesitated as she recalled the many times Sandy had listened to her, given advice, or just encouraged her over the last few months, then she nodded. "Very okay. Sandy's the best adult I know—apart from my dad."

CHAPTER ELEVEN

Dinner was quite noisy that evening as the children, especially Taseu and Wiremu, entertained Professor Bradford and Sandy with stories of their fishing and pig-hunting adventures. Each story was more exaggerated than the last, and when Wiremu described the mad downhill race chasing the wild pig, Taseu laughed so hard that tears squeezed from his eyes and ran down his round cheeks.

"Ow, don't! My stomach's hurting and . . ." He giggled and pressed his cheeks with his hands. "And my cheeks are hurting. Everything's hurting—but it's a good hurt."

Uncle Ammon was laughing too.

"I never heard a pig hunt described quite like that," he said with a chuckle when he was finished eating. "In fact I never realized life on the island could be so funny. You kids are giving me a whole new outlook on life."

His comment only served to encourage Wiremu and Taseu, and they began another story. Only Toni noticed Jerry sitting quietly, not laughing quite as loudly as the others. She wondered what had happened on the island while they had been picking up her father and Sandy from the plane.

After dinner she got the opportunity to be alone with Jerry as they waited for the others to join them for a walk along the beach. Without speaking, they began to walk slowly by the water's edge. Toni finally dug her hands into the pockets of her sweater, took a deep breath, and broke the silence. "Those guys manage to make the smallest thing seem like a huge adventure, don't they?" she asked.

"Mmm." Jerry nodded. "They feed off each other."

"They're fun to be with." Toni lifted her face to the breeze. "They sure make my life interesting . . . and funny."

Jerry frowned slightly. "I guess I'm not used to it," he said. "Wiremu seems a lot different from when we were little. He's a lot louder."

"He's different—or are you different?" Toni asked quietly, then she smiled. "When I saw you two together I thought it'd be weird to have two Wiremus around, but you're not at all the same."

"Is that a good thing?" Jerry asked without looking at her.

Toni didn't hesitate. "Definitely. I'm really enjoying having you all as friends. I thought I'd be lonely when we moved over from Australia, with only Dad and me—without my mother. But I haven't had time to feel like that at all, especially with being part of the Coffin House Kids." She glanced at him. "And it's just like you're part of us, only in a different place."

Jerry didn't say anything, but when he shrugged she could see a slight smile.

"Have you heard from your mother lately?" Toni kept talking as they made their way along a narrow area of rocks at the base of the hill. "You and your dad haven't mentioned her much."

Jerry bent and picked up a small pebble and threw it out in a wide arc over the water. "Dad said she called while we were out fishing the other night." He sunk his hands into the pockets of his long, khaki shorts. "She's probably staying with my nana for another week or so."

"Another week?" Toni looked surprised. "Don't you miss her?"

"Sure." He nodded, then shrugged. "But I think she and Dad are trying to sort things out."

"Haven't they been getting along very well?"

She waited as he took his time answering.

"They get along okay, but they seem to argue a lot lately."

"What about?"

"You ask a lot of questions." He regarded her for a moment, then threw another stone. "They argue about money, about me, about the future."

"Why do they argue about you?" Toni stumbled slightly as a stone rolled beneath her foot.

"I don't know," Jerry said, then he hesitated. "I think it's because I'm probably going to go away to college as a boarding student next year and then they'll be here alone. . . and Dad's been drinking more."

"Does your mum get lonely?" Toni frowned. "I think I would."

"I think it's worse because they don't have very much that they like doing together anymore, and when I go away, it's like there will be nothing left."

Toni watched him pick up a handful of pebbles and throw them in rapid succession. Then he bent over with his hands on his knees and stared at the ground.

"I don't want them to split up," he finally said. "But I can see how Mum feels. It's like Dad loves us, but he can't stop drinking, and that takes him farther away because he feels guilty."

"He hasn't been drinking while we've been here," Toni commented brightly, then she put her head to one side. "Or has he?"

Jerry shook his head. "I don't think he has. I can usually tell, but it hasn't seemed like it. Which is why I get angry at times—because I know he could stop if he tried." He clenched his fists. "If he really wanted to."

"Do you think he drinks because he's worried about money?" Toni asked quietly.

"That might have been why at the beginning," Jerry said, standing up and folding his arms. "Then I think it just became a habit."

"Is he still having money problems?"

There was a long pause, then Jerry turned and stared at her. "You still think my dad's doing something crooked, don't you? To make some money?"

Toni swallowed hard. "I don't know. I only know what I saw, and so far we can't explain it." She stopped and looked right into Jerry's eyes before continuing. "I don't want to see your dad involved in anything he shouldn't be involved in either. I really like him."

Jerry nodded slowly and then sat down on a large rock. "I want to talk to him about it, but it's hard. And right now he's with all the adults."

"Well, that could be a good thing," Toni said with a smile as she sat down near him. "Maybe if he has lots of people who don't drink coming to stay, he might stop."

"And Mum would have more people to talk to, and—"

"And they could start a 'homestay' business or something."

"And Dad might even come back to church," Jerry finished excitedly. Then his shoulders sagged again. "No, that would be asking too much."

Toni sat very still, then she took a deep breath. "I don't think you can ever ask Heavenly Father for too much. I know He listened to me."

Jerry looked straight ahead for a long time. Finally he said very quietly, "I feel funny about doing that."

"Praying?"

"Mmm . . ." He gave a crooked grin. "It's sort of what little kids and old people do. Or some adults."

"Do you think your mum prays?" Toni asked quietly.

"All the time." He turned to her, and she shrugged her shoulders.

"It can't hurt for you to try, and maybe if you actually tell your dad how you feel . . ."

"But I'm the son—he's the father," Jerry objected immediately. "He's supposed to tell me what to do. I can't tell him."

Toni pursed her lips, then repeated in a lower voice. "Maybe . . . if you tell your dad how you feel . . ."

Suddenly they heard Wiremu's voice calling out their names, and they slowly stood up. Neither spoke, then Jerry held out his hand.

"You're a funny girl, Toni, but thanks for listening."

Toni gently shook his hand as if she was greeting him at church, but she knew they had reached a different level of friendship.

"I guess I just want you to be happy, like me," she said with a small smile. "It's taken Dad and me a while, but things got better when we both included Heavenly Father."

"And Sandy?" He grinned. "They look pretty happy together."

"And Sandy."

There was a long pause, and they could hear the others approaching over the rocks behind them. Toni took a quick breath. "Jerry?" she asked. "Did anything happen while you were on the island today? While we were gone?"

"I thought you might ask that." He gave a slow grin, then shook his head. "Taseu and I took the dogs for a walk up the hill, and we watched the boat to see if anything was happening. The dinghy was tied up, so he was on board, but . . ." He shrugged again. "Nothing. Taseu even fell asleep while we waited."

Toni grinned. "Taseu can fall asleep anywhere. The dolphin man probably heard his snoring and laid low."

"I reckon." Jerry smiled as he threw another stone. "I sat there on the hill, and I went over and over in my mind all that's been happening here the last few weeks, and I can't think about anything except that dead guy being found tied to the line. It wasn't our line, so I didn't think about it much, but now I keep wondering if Dad had anything to do with it. And I hate feeling like that." He took a long, deep breath. "In fact, I really don't know what to think right now."

* * *

"I'll drop you at the chapel, and then I have to go down to Tryphena for an appointment and pick some things up off the ferry. I'll be back for you by the time the meetings are over," Uncle Ammon explained as he helped first Sandy, then Toni and Erana, down into the boat. They stepped in carefully in their Sunday dresses and shoes. The boys were already on board, dressed in their long trousers and shirts and ties. It appeared that Uncle Ammon was also trying to fit in with the Sunday spirit, because he was wearing a polo shirt and jeans instead of his usual T-shirt and shorts.

It still seemed strange to Toni to be dressed for church and traveling on a boat, and Professor Bradford was obviously thinking the same thing as he stood above them on the wharf and studied them all with a smile on his face.

"Well, you all scrubbed up very well," he said. "I think I should take a photo for our album—church by boat."

Sandy didn't hesitate to produce her camera. "They won't believe me when I show them this at home, so take two."

Toni watched her dad ponder for a moment, then he focused the camera and quickly took two pictures before stepping onto the boat. She noticed that he frowned a little when he handed the camera back to Sandy.

"I don't like it when you talk about going home," he said.

"Me neither." Wiremu shook his head in agreement and rolled his eyes. "We might have to have Mr. Martin as our basketball coach."

"Of course." Professor Bradford grunted as he moved farther onto the boat. "That's exactly what I was thinking."

The water was rough, and the boat rolled from wave to wave, but the sun was still shining when they landed at Fitzroy and then jumped into the large four-wheel-drive that Uncle Ammon kept parked at the dock.

"I didn't realize the chapel was this near to the airfield," Erana commented, craning her neck to see out the window as they traveled down the winding road again. "I didn't see it yesterday."

"We were busy," Toni said with a glance in the rearview mirror at her father and Sandy sitting together in the backseat. She was getting used to seeing them together, and it kept giving her a warm feeling around her heart that she couldn't remember having before. It felt comfortable—and right.

There were only about twenty people in the small, cream-colored building, even with their entire group attending, but the welcome from everybody was enthusiastic and friendly.

Erana glanced around. "I wonder if Jerry gets lonely here as well," Erana said with a glance around. "I think he's the only one his age here—apart from us."

Wiremu nodded. "He said he'll be the first deacon here for a long time when he turns twelve." He grinned. "You'd really have to do your duties properly for the sacrament wouldn't you—there's no one else to blame."

Taseu leaned forward in his seat. "I reckon you'd really want to do everything right here because everybody knows you so well."

Toni looked at Jerry. The branch president was talking to him at the front of the room, his hand resting on Jerry's shoulder. Then she glanced out the window as Uncle Ammon's truck pulled out and accelerated up the gravel road.

"It could go the other way, as well," she murmured to herself as she settled back in her own chair.

Her father and Sandy were sitting in the next two chairs, and her father rested his arm along the back of her chair. It felt good, and she smiled up at him and snuggled back under his arm, enjoying the warmth of his being next to her. Then she caught a slight movement out of the corner of her eye and saw him rest his other hand over Sandy's, gently linking their fingers together.

Toni found she was holding her breath for a second, then she breathed out and relaxed against her father. She felt him relax too.

There weren't many people there, but their voices filled the room in a beautiful harmony during the hymns, and the music made a shiver run down Toni's spine. Her father responded by squeezing her shoulder gently. She found that during the sacrament prayer and after, while she waited for the sacrament to be passed to her, she was thinking of Jerry and his father and mother. What would it be like to sit in church without her own father? She closed her eyes tightly and prayed for Jerry . . . and for his dad.

The first speaker was just standing up to talk when the door opened behind them. A few people turned to see who had come in, but Toni was watching the elderly woman at the front, who leaned heavily on a walking stick as she prepared to give her talk.

But when first Wiremu, then Taseu, and then Erana quickly moved over one chair, Toni turned and was able to see the expression on Jerry's face when his father sat down quickly on the seat beside him. For a moment Jerry simply stared as his father sat down and hunched forward, his elbows on his knees and his hands gripped together.

"Good morning, brothers and sisters." The frail voice floated over them and gathered strength as the woman spoke from the small wooden pulpit. "It's so lovely to see you all gathered here with us at Great Barrier Branch today . . . so lovely."

Toni couldn't stop watching Jerry. He slowly took a deep breath and then rested his hand against his father's back. The slight touch seemed to trigger something in Uncle Ammon, and he sat up and turned to his son. With the briefest movement he lifted his head and smiled, then settled back in his chair. Jerry kept his arm resting on the chair behind his father's back, and Toni fought the lump growing in her throat.

* * *

"I guess I believe in miracles," Jerry said with a shake of his head. His father was being greeted by the branch president at the end of the sacrament meeting. "I think I might still pinch myself and find out it's a dream."

"Then you'll have to pinch all of us as well," Toni said, smiling. "We're all seeing him too."

"I wonder what made him come back?" Jerry frowned. "He said he had business in Tryphena, but he wouldn't have even gotten as far as Claris in that time."

They stood quietly as Uncle Ammon walked up to them and then awkwardly stuffed his good hand in his pocket and commented, "You looked a bit surprised in there." He was looking at Toni, but they all knew he was talking to his son. "Did I look that out of place?"

Toni was the one who answered first. "No, not at all, and now I really believe Heavenly Father answers prayers." She saw Jerry look at her in surprise, and her heart was pounding at her own words. Was she really saying this?

Uncle Ammon raised his eyebrows and rocked on his heels, and then he looked straight at his son. "Don't you guys get too many ideas! This is just a trial run, okay?" He raised both shoulders. "I don't know if I can do this, son. I'll need lots of help."

Toni watched Jerry catch his bottom lip between his teeth, then nod. "Always happy to help, Dad." He caught his breath. "And I know Mum will be too."

He hesitated, then tentatively held out his hand toward his father. Uncle Ammon stared at it, then grabbed it and pulled Jerry against his chest with his plastered arm in an awkward but tight hug. He kept his arm around Jerry's shoulders as though scared to let him go.

"Why, Dad?" Jerry stared at the ground, then swallowed hard and looked up at his father. "Why did you come back?"

Toni saw the emotion in Uncle Ammon's face as he shook his head then nodded toward Professor Bradford.

"I think it was seeing you all—together. Erana and Wiremu, and Toni with her Dad and Sandy. I don't know. I just got up the road and suddenly wanted to be back here—with my son." He ran his hand over his eyes. "Trouble is—it feels good right now . . . but there's so much else."

Toni felt her stomach tighten. There were a lot of other things to consider at the moment. She was excited that Uncle Ammon was there with them today, but what about his other problems? He still had to deal with his drinking and whatever it was that was happening with the man from the boat.

Toni watched her father put a hand on Uncle Ammon's shoulder and give it a reassuring pat and then do the same to Jerry. And suddenly she knew. She simply had to help Jerry find out about the dolphin man and get Uncle Ammon on the right track to being with his family forever.

CHAPTER TWELVE

"How about we drop Professor Bradford and Sandy at Fitzroy so they can do their 'research?'" Uncle Ammon suggested. He stood by the door with his hands on his hips and grinned. "And we'll go on out to the Needles and catch some nice big snapper for supper. If we go a bit farther we can probably get some Hapuka." He laughed and held up his hands. "Then you can experience catching some decent-sized fish."

Erana looked at her uncle. "Do you mind if I don't go? Auntie Mere said she would show me how to do some flax weaving—*harakeke,* she called it." She clasped both hands together. "I think I'll be much better at that than at fishing."

"I'll second that," Wiremu muttered under his breath.

Erana heard him and turned to scowl at him. "And I'll ignore that."

"Well, I think that's a good idea." Uncle Ammon looked at his watch. "We'll need to leave in fifteen minutes so that we get the right tide. So everybody hustle."

Toni already had her gear ready, so she walked straight down to the wharf with Wiremu. Since church yesterday, she hadn't had a chance to speak to him without all the others around.

"What do you reckon about Uncle Ammon?" she asked as she selected a life jacket and passed another to Wiremu.

"Thanks." He took his time answering as he pulled the vest on. "What do I reckon about his coming to church, or what do I reckon about all the other stuff?"

"The other stuff," Toni answered promptly. "Has Jerry said anything to you?"

"Nope." He played with the black nylon strap on his vest. "I thought you two were having the big conversations."

Something in the tone of his voice made Toni frown at him. "If you mean while we were waiting for you the other day—yes, we did talk, about his parents." She shook her head. "I'm trying to help him."

"Okay, I know you are." Wiremu shrugged. "So what would he be likely to say to me?"

"I don't know. I just thought boys talk more to each other—and you *are* cousins." Toni folded her arms. "And I only really talked to him once, anyway."

Wiremu held up both hands in surrender. "All right, I take it back," he said. "And no, he hasn't said anything else. In fact, he's been really quiet since church yesterday. I thought he'd be pretty happy that his dad came."

"I think he was, but we still haven't figured out what the deal is with the dolphin man, and Jerry said he wanted to talk to his dad about it."

"Well, maybe he'll get a chance some time today." Wiremu looked up at the sky, where wispy, pale-gray clouds suddenly chilled the sun's warmth. "I sure hope it stays sunny while we're out there. Uncle Ammon says we're going out quite a long way." He paused. "Do you think it's a bit strange that we're going out again, not going to lift any pots? I thought we would be doing much more work, but Uncle Ammon seems happy to take us out a lot to other places."

Toni nodded slowly. "You mean, are we being 'decoys' again?"

"Mmm . . ." Wiremu frowned. "It almost makes me want to stay here and watch the dolphin man's boat and see what he does. I reckon we could track him right around the island."

"Jerry tried that yesterday, but he said nothing happened." She frowned. "I think we might have to try tracking him at night."

They dropped Sandy and Professor Bradford at Port Fitzroy and arranged to meet them back at the dock in five hours. As soon as they reached open water, Uncle Ammon instructed the kids to organize the handlines while he steered the boat past more expanses of rugged coastline.

Toni swayed from side to side with the movement of the boat, but she kept her eyes focused on a lone gull hovering above them. It seemed it was suspended in the air by an unseen string. Now and then it would flap its gray wings, but otherwise it remained virtually motionless as it rode the current of air above the boat.

Suddenly it propelled itself upwards and then turned and dove straight down into the water, its wings against its sides, its head pointed down like an arrow.

Jerry walked back just in time to see it dive. "Someone just got dinner," he remarked.

"Something just *became* dinner." Toni touched her stomach. "It still feels strange to think of eating things that were alive a few seconds ago."

"Well, the fish we catch will be very still by the time we cook them." Jerry handed her a fishing line. "We'll be ready to fish soon, and this'll be a bit different from just being out in the dinghy. You might have to fight for these ones."

She looked at him doubtfully. "How big are they going to be? 'Cause I'm happy to just watch."

Wiremu had been listening and broke into the conversation. "No way. This is a competition, eh Jerry?" He took another line from his cousin. "Do you reckon about a twenty-pounder?"

"That could be a bit optimistic." Jerry held up his two hands about eighteen inches apart. "Probably this big, though—or even a bit bigger."

They passed through the Needles, a chain of pointed rock formations that stood like sentinels at the head of the main island. It was almost an eerie, enclosed feeling to move between the rocks with nothing but the open ocean in front of them. Then Uncle Ammon gave the boat more throttle, and it moved quickly out across the water until he looked around and cut the engine completely. The boat rocked quietly on the swell, although Toni noticed that the size of the waves seemed to have increased since they had left home.

Jerry dropped the large anchor over the side, and it seemed that the rope unraveled for a long time.

"How far down does it have to go?" Taseu asked, peering over the side. "It's going forever."

Uncle Ammon turned the steering wheel slightly. "We're over a rock shelf, so it'll go about two hundred feet."

Taseu whistled through pursed lips. "There's gotta be some fish for us somewhere down there."

"Or giant squid or whales." Wiremu held up his hands and wriggled his fingers.

Uncle Ammon laughed and got ready to throw out a line. "I think we'd have to go a bit deeper than that for giant things, but maybe a whale . . ."

Toni had sat patiently for nearly an hour while the others had pulled fish up amidst all sorts of whoops and yells of victory. The shining snapper lay in a lidded container, although Wiremu took the top off frequently to check that his catch was still the biggest.

"I still reckon two smaller ones outdo one big one," Taseu said with a shake of his head. "They were taking up more ocean space."

"That's one way of looking at it." Uncle Ammon nodded as he held up his hand and checked the sky. "Did you feel that? I think we're getting rained on." He frowned at a large, dark-gray cloud lying low in the sky to their right. "That's come across really quickly. We might need to finish up soon and get back home."

Toni suddenly felt her line strain against her hand, and she almost let it go. "I've got one!" she yelled.

"Hold on!" Jerry grabbed the black line and began to pull it in smoothly while she got control, then he handed it to her, keeping one hand loosely around it. "Just pull it steadily. You've got a lot of line to bring in."

Toni could feel her heart pounding as she pulled hand over hand. Occasionally the line would buck and pull, and it gave her a fright every time.

"This is nerve-wracking," she murmured as she kept her eyes totally focused on the water around the line.

Taseu leaned right over the side of the boat so he could be the first to see the fish as it came up. "Here it is!" he called. "It's huge!"

As it neared the surface of the water, the large fish twisted and pulled, and the line slipped through Toni's fingers. Again, Jerry grabbed it and held on tight while he got his other hand past Toni's.

"Keep pulling!" He gave the brisk order, and she tightened her grip.

"Nearly there!" Uncle Ammon encouraged them from behind as Jerry let go. Toni gave one last pull, and the fish flopped over the side of the boat. It lay still on the floor for a second, then heaved and flipped several inches.

"I think you win, Toni." Wiremu couldn't keep the admiration out of his voice. "I hate to admit it, but I think you win."

"I know she wins," Taseu countered. He leaned forward to pick up the fish by its tail and nearly leaped as far as the fish when it started flipping again. "Cut that out!" he yelled and the others laughed, and then he joined in. "I can't believe I just told a fish off."

They pulled up all of the lines, and Uncle Ammon started the boat immediately to head back toward the Needles. The fishing forgotten, Toni watched as the gray cloud seemed to move directly toward them, becoming a solid wall that extended right down to the water.

As it moved, the waves around the boat became more erratic and choppy, their tops cresting against the boat and even sending a heavy spray across the floor.

"Everybody got their life jackets on properly?" Uncle Ammon called from the cabin as the children all held firmly onto their seats. "We should be able to outrun it, but it could get a bit choppy."

Nobody talked as the waves seemed to get bigger and bigger. Soon the water started falling in heavy splatters onto the boat, and Toni's initial thrill at the moving waves gradually changed to a knot in her stomach. Then suddenly the rain changed to heavy pellets, beating onto the deck around them and onto their bodies. She felt Jerry's hand on her shoulder.

"You need to go up under the bow. You'll keep dry there." He pointed into the cabin toward the front of the boat. "Just stay on the seats. We'll be out of this soon."

They could still feel the pitching of the boat as it tackled the waves, and sometimes Toni was lifted right off the seat when they went up with a wave and then crashed back down. She could see Uncle Ammon concentrating hard and fighting to control the wheel with his good hand. Jerry stood silently in the cabin beside him, his feet braced against the movement of the boat.

"Toni's fish!" Jerry suddenly exclaimed. He ran to the cabin door. "We forgot to bring it down!"

"Don't worry about . . ." Uncle Ammon's words were lost in the noise of the wind and sea as his son worked his way out onto the deck. Toni waited, her fingers gripping the upholstered seat, until she saw his legs appear through the doorway again. Then, just as quickly, he was gone.

"Jerry!" She heard Uncle Ammon cry out and saw the tortured expression on his face as he struggled to hold the wheel while looking out for his son.

"What's happened?" Wiremu was on his feet instantly and trying to hold on so he could move up to the doorway, but he kept stumbling with the movement of the boat.

"Wiremu, take the wheel. Just hold it tight in the same place!" Uncle Ammon's voice was a ragged yell, and Wiremu kept moving forward, bracing himself against the doorjamb until he was holding onto the steering wheel, his teeth gritted tightly together. Uncle Ammon was gone in an instant, his body blurring into the wash of salt spray. Taseu was right behind, but he stopped at the door.

"Jerry's hurt," Taseu barely whispered as he glanced back toward Toni. His face was drained of color. "I can't see him."

Toni felt as if a cold hand had gripped her heart and twisted it. She put her hand to her mouth to stop the instant feeling of nausea that swept through her body, and she fought to keep the tears from her eyes. Her first reaction was to get up and go to the deck, but Taseu held up his hand.

"Hang on. Get back!" He stepped backward as Uncle Ammon appeared in the opening, the water streaming off his clothes as he pulled Jerry's totally limp body down the short stairway.

"Help me get him onto the seat!" Uncle Ammon's instruction was brisk, and the children moved immediately. Taseu moved right back to take Jerry's shoulders, and Toni helped ease his legs up onto the seat.

It was a shock to see Jerry's normally healthy face almost completely drained of color except for the trickle of red blood that ran down past his ear from a cut on his head. His neck was at an odd angle, and as Uncle Ammon straightened it cautiously with both hands, Toni gasped.

"He's bleeding at the back as well!" she exclaimed, pointing at the pool of blood that was spreading across the fabric of the seat under Jerry's head.

Uncle Ammon put his hand up to the back of Jerry's head. His hand came away covered in blood.

"Taseu! Grab the first-aid kit under the front seat!" he ordered. "Quickly!"

Taseu had the white plastic box out and the lid open before he'd even finished speaking.

"Find anything we can make a pad with to stop the bleeding." Uncle Ammon reached into the box with his other hand for a large bandage while the children looked around quickly.

"My other T-shirt!" Toni rocked with the boat and reached for her small backpack containing an extra shirt and her swimming suit. She fumbled slightly with the catch but quickly handed Ammon the T-shirt.

"Perfect!" He rolled it and placed it over the wound on the back of Jerry's head and firmly wrapped the bandage around it several times. Before he'd finished the bandaging, a faint red stain appeared from the wound on Jerry's fore-head, but they could see it easing up a bit.

The children watched silently as Uncle Ammon held his two fingers against Jerry's throat, then he nodded and breathed deeply. "He's okay. His pulse is strong, but his head's sure taken a beating."

"What happened?" Toni managed to get the words out. "Why did he go out?"

Uncle Ammon gave her a lopsided smile as he moved quickly to take over from Wiremu. "He was trying to save your fish."

CHAPTER THIRTEEN

"Man, that gave me a fright yesterday." Wiremu sat down on his branch of the tree and wrapped his arms around his knees. "I don't think I've ever seen so much blood."

Toni nodded in agreement. "I was so scared. Do you really think he's all right?"

"Uncle Ammon said he was going to be fine," Erana stated firmly. "Those head cuts always bleed a lot because the vessels are close to the surface, but they checked for concussion and it's not too bad."

"Since when have you become the nurse?" Wiremu asked, pulling a face at her.

"Since you all stopped listening properly. The doctor explained it all, and he must have said Jerry was all right a hundred times." She glared at her cousin, then immediately looked sorry. "I mean, I know it must have been awful out in the storm, but is it any use going over it again and again?"

Toni looked at her friend gratefully. "Erana's right. We have been kind of repeating ourselves a bit. Jerry is going to be okay."

"But it'll make a great story at school," Taseu put in quickly. "I've got dibs on telling it first."

"It'll make a great fish story." Wiremu grinned and held his arms outstretched as far as they could reach. "How the biggest snapper nearly got away."

Toni threw a small lump of clay at his shoulder. "You're going to get into trouble with your exaggerating one day," she said.

"Speaking of trouble." Taseu suddenly dropped his voice to a whisper. "There's the dolphin man."

They all quickly dropped down behind the lower branch as the stranger appeared on the deck of his boat. He was wearing the same jacket he'd worn on the ferry, along with dark trousers and a cap pulled down over his face. They watched him check the equipment.

"I think he's leaving!" Wiremu muttered under his breath. "Look, he's pulling in the anchor."

"Where do you think he's going?" Taseu whispered again.

"To poach someone else's fish," Wiremu said, shaking his head. "It really ticks me off that we couldn't pin anything on that guy."

"But if we did, we might be getting Uncle Ammon in trouble as well," Toni said quietly, watching the boat as it cruised out of the bay. "Maybe this man will just go away."

"And Uncle Ammon won't do anything stupid again because he's trying to do the right things now." Erana smiled. "I like the way that story ends."

When they lost sight of the boat around the cliff, Wiremu sat back and frowned. "But stories don't always end happily. They sometimes end with people learning a lesson."

"So do you still think we should try to find out?" Toni dug the end of her sandal under a piece of root and looked doubtful. "I think I just want to forget about poachers and help Jerry get better."

* * *

The light in the room was quite dim, because the curtains were almost completely drawn. Toni had to blink a couple of times so her eyes could adjust from the bright sunlight outside.

"I thought I was the one having trouble seeing anything," Jerry said from the bed. "Don't tell me you got hit on the head as well."

"Oh, no—it's just the light, I mean the light outside, not inside." Toni stammered as she focused on the white bandage wrapped around Jerry's head. It seemed to look more serious than the one they'd hastily applied on the boat. She screwed up her nose. "Does it still really hurt?"

"Nope, I can't really feel anything." Jerry grinned, then winced slightly and touched his forehead. "Well, maybe sometimes."

"So how long do you have to stay in bed?" Toni remained standing a few feet away.

"Not long." Jerry eased himself up on his pillows. "I'll be up tomorrow for sure. The doctor said to just rest today and then take it easy for the next few days."

"But we'll be going home on Thursday!" Toni protested, then put her hand to her mouth. "Not that that makes any difference . . . I mean, you just have to get better."

Jerry waved his hand. "I'll be fine. Dad said we're going to have a nice safe day off over at Whangapoua on Wednesday and then go up to the hot springs."

"But don't you have to walk through the bush to the hot springs?" Toni asked, frowning. "You won't be . . ."

"I'll be fine." Jerry touched his bandage again. "This is a tough island head."

"So how's the patient?" Uncle Ammon walked in, closely followed by Taseu and Wiremu. Erana came in right behind them with Professor Bradford and Sandy.

"We just thought we'd see how many people we can fit into the room." Professor Bradford held his daughter by the shoulders and shuffled over to make room for the others. "We came to sing to you."

They all laughed at the alarmed look on Jerry's face.

"Just kidding." Wiremu grinned. "We want you to get better, not make you worse."

"Actually, I asked everybody to come in," Uncle Ammon said quietly and sat down on the edge of his son's bed. "Seeing how everybody here has had a part to play in this." He hesitated, and Toni felt her father's hand on her arm.

"Yesterday, during the storm . . ." Ammon swallowed hard and exhaled a deep breath. "During that stupid storm that I didn't read well enough, I had to struggle to keep the boat steady, and it really took all I had. Even though Jerry knows how to drive the boat, I knew I was the only one with the experience to get us through the storm, but my arm made me feel like a cripple, and then . . ." He swallowed again. "Then when Jerry got hurt, I felt completely helpless."

There was a long silence, and nobody moved.

"I was so grateful that you children were able to help Jerry and get him comfortable." He pretended to hit Jerry on the arm. "I kept thinking he'd get up soon and it would all be all right. But he didn't, and that was when I started praying." He lowered his head and nodded. "I hadn't even thought to until then because I'm so used to handling things on my own, but I realized that I couldn't do that anymore."

"It must have worked, eh, Dad?" Jerry plucked at the bed sheet and attempted a grin. "I'm still here."

Ammon looked up. "Something sure worked." He cleared his throat. "I also realized that that was pretty much what I was doing with my whole life. I was doing my own thing and thinking that I was taking responsibility for my family, but I haven't been thinking about their happiness—our happiness." He shrugged as he pointed around at all of them. "You have all helped me realize what I've been missing and how I was really messing up. I guess I just wanted to thank you." He patted his hands on his thighs as if suddenly embarrassed by his confession. "That's it."

Nobody spoke for a time, then, as usual, it was Wiremu who broke the silence. "Well, heck," he said, folding his arms and looking around at everybody proudly. "And we thought we were just coming over to help you with the fishing."

* * *

"Toni!" Jerry beckoned her from the doorway to the kitchen. "I need to talk to you."

"Right now?" She glanced at him and back to the pile of dishes that she was drying while Sandy did the washing.

Sandy waved her away with a sudsy finger. "That's fine. I can finish up."

"Thanks, Sandy." Toni quickly dried her hands and hung the dish towel over the wall rack. Jerry was already walking out to the path.

"What's the matter?" she asked as he began to walk down to the wharf ahead of her. It was only Wednesday morning, but he was walking around easily.

"I just wanted to tell you that I had a talk with Dad last night." When they reached the end of the wharf, he turned and sat down with his legs dangling over the edge.

"What about?" Toni asked cautiously as she sat down beside him.

"Lots of things, really." He stared out at the water. "He'd just been talking to Mum."

"Oh." She stole a look sideways at him. "What happened? Didn't she know about your accident?"

"Yeah, he'd already told her about my accident the night before, but this time he told her that he was stopping drinking and that he was coming back to church . . . that he'd already been back to church with us on Sunday."

"Oh my goodness." Toni found she was hardly breathing. "What did she say?"

Jerry grinned, clasped his hands together and rested his elbows on his knees. Toni noted that he looked like his father when he sat like that.

"Dad said she cried, and then she tried to talk, but she kept on crying." Jerry pretended to look confused. "I think she must have been happy."

Toni couldn't stop the smile, then she gave a little laugh. "That makes me feel happy. It works on everybody, doesn't it?"

"It sure does." He smiled. "Then we talked about his giving up drinking, and he said he's thrown out every bit of alcohol, and then he asked me to help him learn about being a priesthood holder. He said that with me nearly becoming a deacon, we're about at the same level, so we can learn together." His hands tightened on each other. "Imagine me and my dad passing the sacrament together. That'll be so cool."

Toni watched him smile thoughtfully, then he turned his head and held up one finger. "But there's one other thing we talked about."

Toni stared at his finger, and she could feel an icy coldness touch her spine. She had been trying to block out any thought of Uncle Ammon's involvement in anything bad, but now her doubts came back as soon as Jerry even suggested the idea.

"Dolphin Man?" It was barely a whisper.

"Dolphin Man," Jerry repeated quietly. "I told Dad straight out what you'd seen down at the wharf the other night and how we couldn't figure why he would deny knowing the guy when he was going out with him in the dinghy at night."

"And what did he say?" Toni almost didn't want to hear the answer.

"He took a long time to say anything." Jerry leaned back with his arms behind him and looked straight at Toni. "Finally he looked right at me and asked me if I trusted him."

"And?"

Jerry gave a weak grin. "I tell you, it took me a while to answer, but I told him that I did." He shrugged. "Then he said that I really had to trust him on this one and that he'd be able to fill me in soon."

"That was it?" Toni felt mildly disappointed. "Nothing else?"

Jerry shook his head. "Nothing else, but Toni—" He smiled. "I really do trust him."

CHAPTER FOURTEEN

"I can't believe we leave Great Barrier tomorrow." Erana held up a small woven flax bag. "I only just got to finish my first *kite* and I want to do lots more. Auntie Mere said I have real talent."

"Maybe your grandma knows someone who can teach you back home," Toni suggested. She finished tying the laces on her sneakers and stood up. "I think your weaving looks so good, but I don't know that I could ever do it."

Erana sat down on the edge of the bed and stared at Toni. "It's funny how we can be friends and yet be so different, eh?" She giggled. "You want to do all the things that the boys do and I want to do everything they don't—except basketball . . . and athletics."

"See, we do some things the same." Toni smiled. "I don't know why I don't like sitting still to do crafty type things. I really like them when you do them, but I think I've always been too clumsy—my hands get in the way instead of doing what they're told."

Erana nodded knowingly. "Sandy said the same thing when I showed her. You two are so much alike." She pretended to study the small piece of paua shell she had attached to the handle of the bag. "Do you think she and your dad will get married?"

Toni paused in the middle of pulling her hooded sweatshirt over her head. The same thought had been going through her mind a lot since her father had arrived on the island, and her feelings had gone from nervous excitement at the idea to a deep concern that made her stomach knot.

"I don't know." She pulled her sleeves down slowly. "I know he really likes her, and he's always really happy when they're together."

"But would you mind if they got married?" Erana crossed her legs up onto the bed and leaned forward with her chin in her hands. "I think it would be so romantic."

Married! Toni silently mouthed the one word she had avoided thinking about. She had forced herself to accept the idea of her father and her coach dating, and it had been a lot easier because they all attended church as well, but married?

"Have you even thought about that?" Erana persisted. "That would make Sandy your mother."

"I realize that," Toni answered abruptly, then her shoulders slumped. "I'm sorry, Erana—I just haven't really thought that far."

"I think it would be so cool." Erana picked up her pillow and cuddled it. "If my dad ever got married I'd like it to be to someone like Sandy." She hesitated. "Then again, it would be better if she did crafty type things."

"Who, Sandy?" Toni looked puzzled.

"No, Dad's new wife." Erana rolled her eyes. "Like he's even looking for one!"

"I didn't think my dad was looking for one— a wife, I mean." Toni sat down on the bed beside her friend. "I thought it was just going to always be him and me. We've even got used to my mother not being around."

Erana hugged the pillow tighter. "I can't even remember my mum hardly. It's always just been me and Wiremu and Grandma—and Dad when he came home from traveling."

"He's home a lot more now, though." Toni glanced at Erana. "He might start going out with somebody—then what would you do?"

Erana looked up at the ceiling, then she giggled. "That's when I come and ask you for help. You can do it all first."

* * *

Whangapoua Beach swung out to the left of them in a wide, creamy-white arc that seemed lighter because of the swell of dark bush that rose up behind the sand. A light wind was tipping the blue-green waves so that whitecaps rolled along their tops as they came into shore.

"It looks good for surfing," Uncle Ammon said, pointing out at the waves. "This beach has one of the best right-hand bars in the country."

"Meaning?" Erana always seemed to ask the questions the others wanted to ask.

"The waves break from right to left," Jerry explained, sweeping his arm in the same direction. "And it's not too rough today."

"I've just got to go down to Claris for a bit, so I could drop you down at Awana Beach or Medlands if you want." Uncle Ammon glanced back at them. "But Jerry wanted to take you flounder spotting as well."

"No, we'll stay here." Jerry picked up his surfboard. "We can surf now and go up the estuary when the tide's lower."

Taseu and Wiremu didn't need any more encouragement, and they raced each other down the sand toward the water. Just like always,

Wiremu hurled himself into the waves and came up swimming frantically for a few strokes, while Taseu ran in up to his knees and then stood still as the cold water hit him. Jerry soon joined them, but Erana and Sandy walked down to the high-tide mark and began looking for shells. Toni spread her beach towel on the sand and sat down to watch.

"Aren't you going in?" Her father settled himself beside her and adjusted his wide-brimmed canvas hat.

"Not yet." Toni wrapped her arms around her knees. "I like to get really hot first, then go in." She raised one finger briefly. "And the boys have the boards. I'll wait for one of them to get tired."

"You're going to try surfing?" Her father looked surprised. "You haven't done that before, have you?"

"Not really." Toni smiled. "Not with waves anyway. We've been playing around on the boards in the bay at home." She shook her head. "I mean, at the island."

"Already thinking of it as home?" Professor Bradford nodded. "Sandy was saying that the other day."

"About the island?" Toni looked surprised.

"No . . . about New Zealand." Her father stared out at the ocean from under the brim of his hat. "She really likes it here."

Toni sat quietly for a long moment, then she began to make a figure eight in the sand with her finger. "I think she really likes you—maybe more than New Zealand."

She couldn't look at her father, but she could sense him holding his breath.

"You think she does?" he asked quietly.

"Uh-huh." Toni pressed her finger into the middle of the shape and twisted it slowly. "Erana and I were talking about it this morning."

"Oh? And what did you and Erana decide?" She could hear the smile in his voice, and it made her heart feel warm.

"I said . . ." Toni hesitated and pressed her finger down harder. "I said that you're always really happy when Sandy's around. You are, aren't you?"

"Uh-huh . . ." Her father turned and rested on his elbow so he could see her face. "Does that make you happy?"

Toni squinted her eyes and looked straight ahead. She just couldn't look at her father yet. "Yes, I guess so." She brushed the sand off her hands and leaned forward against her knees. "Erana asked me how I would feel if you got married."

"Oh, she did, did she?" He sounded surprised, then he gave a slight chuckle. "She's never one to hold back with the questions, is she?"

Toni giggled, and then they both went quiet.

"How *would* you feel, chickie?" His voice was low, and she knew she had to look at him. She turned slowly, and beneath the brim of his hat she could see his warm gray eyes with a hint of moisture in them. She suddenly knew that whatever she said now would determine the decision he made.

"Do you ever think about Mum?" She watched him carefully. He raised both eyebrows as if the question surprised him, then he nodded.

"Sometimes—when I look at you. You're like her in many ways." He held up his hand. "All the good ways."

Toni smiled. They had spent many hours talking since her mother had left them—hours of getting to know each other and sharing their plans for the future. Plans that had only ever included the two of them.

"I've been thinking a lot about my career—my plans for the future." She swallowed with difficulty. "Sandy and I were talking about it."

"Your career?" Her father looked confused at the turn of conversation, but he nodded. "That's important."

"Yes, well . . . I really want to do something with animals, and Sandy said I should be thinking about it now." She wriggled her toes down into the sand. "And then I got to thinking that in only a few years I'll be wanting to do my career and everything, and then you'll be all alone."

"Of course." Professor Bradford nodded, beginning to understand what she was saying. "So you're planning to leave me alone in my old age?"

"Well, I don't want to." Toni patted sand over the hole she'd made. "But it might be better if you had company—then you wouldn't be lonely."

"I see." Her father smiled. "And do you think Sandy would be good company for me—in my old age?"

Toni finally looked straight at him and nodded seriously. "I think so. You could play basketball together and do research and stuff."

"Sounds good." He sat up and rested his hand on her shoulder. "But how would my daughter feel if we had Sandy's company sooner rather than later?"

"Mmm . . ." Toni rested her cheek against her father's hand and closed her eyes briefly, then she nodded. "Your daughter would think that's a very good idea—'cause then you'd be happy all the time, and Wiremu would be jealous because I'd have my own basketball coach living at home."

Her father burst out laughing, pulled her close and gave her the longest hug before kissing the top of her head. "So I have your permission?" he asked.

"Absolutely." Toni grinned. "When are you going to ask her?"

"Now that is the next question." Her father moved closer and dropped his voice to a whisper. "I think I may need your help on that part."

* * *

"What were you and your dad talking about?" Jerry pushed himself up to a sitting position and straddled his surfboard. The white bandage on his head had been replaced by a large band-aid, and he looked healthy and fit resting on his surfboard beside Toni just beyond the swell.

"Oh, marriage and stuff like that," Toni answered casually. She was trying to get into the same position as he was in, but her board kept tipping underneath her.

"For real?" Jerry reached over and held the board for her while she got situated.

"Yep." Toni reached her hands out on either side of the board and paddled in the water. It felt cool and fresh, and she raised her face to the sun. It felt like nothing could go wrong the way she was feeling with the sun, sky, and surf surrounding her. "He really likes Sandy."

"Then it looks like we've both got what we wanted, eh?" Jerry dribbled some water over his leg with his hand. The water formed into small drops that glistened against his brown skin. "My dad's coming back to church, and your dad's . . ." He hesitated. "Has he asked her yet?"

Toni shook her head. "Not yet. We were just working that out."

"Together?" Jerry looked surprised, then he nodded. "That's pretty cool."

"It is. Whoops." Toni swung a bit to the side as a wave swelled beneath her and lifted the board. Jerry steadied her again, then he swung his feet back and lay down on his stomach on his board.

"Let's go in, and I'll show you how to chase flounder." He began to paddle one hand after the other in strong strokes that Toni watched carefully then copied.

"Has your dad said anything more about the dolphin man?" She made an effort to keep up with him.

"Nope, nothing." Jerry glanced over his shoulder. "But he will. I'm positive."

* * *

They spent the better part of an hour in the smooth-flowing water of the estuary, chasing the baby flounder that lay in the murky stretches of sand just below the surface. There was something exciting about sneaking up on the very flat, leathery fish with eyes on the top of their heads. It looked as if they could see in all directions. Then, having them scuttle off through the sand gave such a good fright.

"Ohh!" Erana squealed as a baby fish wiggled off just below her hand. "That was so close!"

"You always say it's close, and it's miles away!" Wiremu stood knee-deep in the water with his hands on his hips, his eyes darting back and forth to detect the fish.

"I've got one!" Taseu yelled, holding up a fiercely flipping fish barely larger than his hand. "Ahh!" he yelped again as it whipped out of his hand and plunged back into the water. He fell down right behind it.

"It was tiny anyway." Wiremu looked unimpressed, then he grinned. "You probably flattened one when you sat down."

They all laughed as Taseu rolled to one side and ran his hand across the ground underneath him. "Nope." He chuckled, then lunged forward in the water, creating a wall of spray as he saw another fish.

They never caught anything, but Jerry assured them that wasn't the point. It was the stalking and chasing that was the real fun. They finally sank down on the bank of the estuary, exhaustion and sunburn the only rewards for their efforts.

"I'm so thirsty I could drink the river dry," Wiremu complained. "Do you think your dad will be back soon?"

Jerry frowned and looked back toward the road. "He should have been back ages ago. He said he just had to check something at Claris." He shrugged. "I don't know where he is."

Toni sat quietly. She tried to get the image of Uncle Ammon sneaking down to the wharf in the dark of night out of her mind, but it still bothered her occasionally. She bit her lip. Jerry trusted his father, so she must try to as well. He seemed like a good man, and he was obviously trying to do the right thing.

A few minutes later Uncle Ammon swung the truck to a halt on the side of the road. "Sorry to keep you waiting!" he called out. "I've got a picnic ready, and if you feel like a walk, we'll take it up to the hot springs!"

"A walk!" Taseu rolled his tongue out of his mouth and looked exhausted.

"Hot springs?" Erana fanned herself with her hand. "I'm boiling already."

"Hey, you'll love them." Jerry was already on his feet. "And it's so cool in the bush you won't be hot once you get there."

"In the bush?" Wiremu frowned as he picked up his towel and shook the sand off it. "Who'd build hot pools in the bush?"

After parking the truck, they walked for half an hour in the bush. Their trek along paths bordered by the low-hanging branches of towering trees and thick native bush *was* cool and peaceful. Long, winding tree limbs covered with brilliant, waxy leaves of every shade of green wove themselves into a canopy that protected the hikers from the afternoon sun.

"Here you are." Ammon pointed downwards with his plaster-casted arm. A plateau below them surrounded a steaming pool that had been naturally formed out of the rock.

Wiremu looked around. "These are the pools? I thought we were going to swimming pools."

"These are the swimming pools." Uncle Ammon grinned and swung his backpack off his shoulder. "Natural pools provided by Heavenly Father. If we keep walking up the trail, there's a whole bunch at different temperatures. We can keep going to the really hot one if you want."

Jerry climbed back onto the trail. "I reckon we stay here," he said. "This one holds more people, and there's a place to eat our picnic."

At the mention of the picnic, Toni glanced quickly at her father and saw him respond with a slight smile and a nod. "A picnic sounds good to me." He removed a backpack full of food from his back. "I'm ready to try those *paua* fritters."

It was quite a feast when they had spread out all the food and drinks, and Wiremu patted his stomach happily. "I never thought I'd say it, but I think I'm going to miss all this seafood when we go home. Even the mussel sandwiches."

Toni wrinkled up her nose. "I'm not with you on that one. I'll stick with crayfish and fish and chips."

"Well, who wants to try some fritters?" Her father reached for a plastic container filled with dark, rounded shapes. Then he hesitated and reached back into the backpack. "Or we could be really brave and try the original. Toni, do you want to be the first?"

He held out a rounded shell that fit into the palm of his hand. It was whitish-gray all over and its surface was rough and ridged. Toni looked at her father briefly, then hesitantly took the shell from him. She made as if to open it, then quickly passed it toward Sandy.

"No, I think Sandy should try it. It can be a memory of New Zealand."

Sandy raised one eyebrow and held out her hand. "I have to be brave? What sort of memory is that going to be?" She wrinkled her nose and sniffed at the shell. "The smell's enough of a memory."

"Go on, Sandy." Ammon grinned and passed her a knife. "With *paua,* you'll either love it or you'll hate it."

They all watched as Sandy took the knife and began to ease it through the slight opening that joined the two parts of the shell. Immediately, it opened in her hands, and she caught it before it dropped.

"Oh my goodness!" She held the two parts of the shell in both hands, then her eyes grew wide and she stared at the half in her right hand. "Oh, my goodness," she repeated quietly, then slowly looked up at the professor.

"What's wrong?" Toni's dad asked, and Toni held her breath. "Don't you like *paua*?"

Everybody was quiet, but they were not sure why until Sandy finally moved and held the two shells apart in her lap.

"I think paua is beautiful," she responded softly. "But not quite what I expected."

"It's a ring!" Erana nearly fell forward as the slimmest ray of sunlight came through the trees and reflected off the inside of the shell. "There's a diamond ring inside!"

Toni felt her heart flutter as she stared at the slim gold band with a bright, glistening diamond on top. It sparkled brilliantly against the rich cobalt-blue and turquoise-green swirls of the paua shell. It looked beautiful—exactly as she and her father had planned.

Sandy still held the shell, and they all waited as she slowly put it down and picked up the ring.

"Are you going to put it on?" Erana finally whispered, her eyes still wide with excitement.

"Should I?" Sandy looked up at Toni and waited until she nodded enthusiastically.

Slowly, Sandy held it out to the professor. Toni watched as he looked deep into Sandy's eyes then took the ring from her. He held it for a second, then slid it onto her finger.

"Does this mean you're getting married?" Taseu asked breathlessly. "Will you still be our coach?"

"Of course she will." Wiremu sat back with a nod of satisfaction as Professor Bradford hugged his new fiancée and then his daughter. "But she might have to take the ring off to practice."

CHAPTER FIFTEEN

"I don't know about you, but I'm exhausted." Taseu hung his lifejacket on the hook in the shed, then stood aside so the others could hang theirs. "Surfing, swimming, floundering, hot pools, wedding rings . . . all in one day!"

"It's not a wedding ring," Erana corrected him immediately as she followed him out of the shed. "It's an engagement ring."

"Same difference." He shrugged. "They both mean Toni gets a new mum."

Wiremu thumped Taseu on the shoulder. "And we keep our coach. It's a good arrangement. I almost can't wait to get back to school."

"School!" Taseu stopped abruptly at the bottom of the stairs to the veranda, put his hands on his hips, and stared at Wiremu. "I had come this close to forgetting about school," he said, holding his finger and thumb closely together. "Why did you have to remind me?"

"Well, something might have occurred to you when we got on the plane tomorrow." Wiremu shook his head. "Or we could just leave you here."

"That could be an idea." Taseu nodded and held his hands up in the air as if he were driving. "Jerry and I could drive the boat to school—no lessons if it's windy—fish and chips every day . . ."

"And no shops to go get ice cream or fizzy drinks—not that you should be doing that anyway—and no basketball." Wiremu added as Jerry came down the front steps.

"Okay, you've convinced me." Taseu shook his head. "Sorry, Jerry, I won't be staying on the island."

"What?" Jerry frowned then nodded. "Oh . . . right. Oh, well, maybe next year. You can still come and visit, though." He stopped and looked around at them all. "Yeah, that'd be good. I'd really like you all to come and stay again."

Erana sat down on the stair and folded her arms across her knees. "I can't believe how much we've done in just a week. I feel like we've been here for ages."

Toni sat down beside her, and the boys sat down on the grass and on the lower steps. Nobody felt like moving as the sun dropped behind the hill at the back of the house and the first evening chill cooled the air.

Wiremu lay on his back, and Rima was by him in a second, gently licking his cheek.

"Hey, Rima." He rubbed the sides of her neck with his hands. "Have we left you alone all day?" He dodged another kiss. "How are you going to like being without your playmate, eh?"

Toni watched Rima flop down beside Miner under the large tree beside the veranda.

She smiled. "I'll bet she'll miss him," she said, watching the dogs roll and playfully bite at each other. "I'm going to be boring company in comparison."

Suddenly both dogs leaped to their feet, began barking, and then raced off down the path to the wharf.

"Visitors." Jerry stood up and brushed off his shorts. "Dad!" he called into the house. "Were you expecting anyone?"

Uncle Ammon came to the doorway with a box in his hands. "Possibly." He glanced at his watch and frowned, then slowly lowered the box onto a chair and took a deep breath. "You all just wait here. I'll go see who it is."

The dogs were still barking down at the wharf when he walked past them, and then the children heard his sharp command for the dogs to be still. There was instant silence. None of the children spoke as they listened.

"What are we listening for?" Taseu whispered. "We can't hear anything from here."

"True." Erana nodded. "But your dad seemed worried, Jerry. Is anything wrong?"

Jerry shrugged his shoulders and shook his head. "Not that I know of." He looked at Toni. "He usually tells me if he's expecting someone."

They waited quietly. Suddenly both of the dogs came running back around the corner of the shed, then circled back down the path again. "Whoever's here must be coming up to the house," Jerry commented and stood up again. Just then two figures appeared around the corner.

Uncle Ammon walked with his head down, and the man behind him in a dark blue uniform shirt with epaulets on the shoulders held him firmly by the shoulder. He wore a dark cap that shaded his face, but he looked up when he and Uncle Ammon stopped a few feet in front of the children.

"The dolphin man!" Wiremu whispered as all of them recognized the man from the ferry—the stranger they'd watched loitering around the bays for the last few days—the stranger who now had Uncle Ammon apparently under arrest . . . or something.

Uncle Ammon still had his head down, and Toni felt a rush of pity for Jerry as she saw him staring at his father. The man's hand was still on

Uncle Ammon's shoulder, and she saw his fingers tighten. Then Ammon looked up. She could see the sparkle in his eyes that made him look so much like his son, and she felt an instant mixture of relief and confusion when he stepped back and held his hand out toward the stranger.

"Dolphin Man, I'd like to introduce you to our newest island detectives—otherwise known as the Coffin House Kids from Beach Haven." He pointed to each of the children in turn. "Toni, Erana, Wiremu, Taseu, and, of course, you know about my son, Jerry."

The man tipped the brim of his cap at them, and Uncle Ammon turned back toward him.

"Well, it's sure good to meet you all—officially. I'm Dan Maddison, and I'm an officer from the Ministry of Fisheries." He took his cap off and nodded toward Uncle Ammon. "I hear I have some explaining to do."

"Ministry of Fisheries," Toni repeated. She wasn't sure what it was, but it sounded official, and she could see from the look on Jerry's face that he was relieved, so she relaxed as well.

Uncle Ammon smiled and gestured for Dan to sit down on the stairs.

Just then Professor Bradford and Sandy walked out from the kitchen. "What's happening out here?" Professor Bradford asked, glancing around but not noticing the taller figure at the side until Taseu pointed accusingly at Dan.

"This is the dolphin man."

Dan smiled and looked around at the children. "I hear I've been called a few names over the last week. I've come to tell you all what's been happening and to clear up some . . . rumors." He raised an eyebrow at Toni, and she felt the heat rush through her cheeks and ears.

Now that he was sitting in front of her in his uniform, she began to regret every doubtful thought she'd ever had about him and Uncle Ammon.

"First of all, I want to thank you all for being so observant about what was happening around the island." Dan gestured toward Uncle Ammon. "When Jerry told his father what you had all seen and what you suspected about him and about me, I was amazed at how quickly you'd become aware of things looking suspicious."

Uncle Ammon nodded and held up his broken arm. "I thought I was just getting some fishing helpers—not a bunch of detectives."

"Detectives?" Professor Bradford interrupted with a puzzled look. "What's been happening?"

Dan touched the epaulette on his shoulder. "Officially, I'm the detective. I'm an officer with the Ministry of Fisheries, and I came out here to do a bit of undercover investigating about some poaching that's been going on."

Wiremu's eyes bulged. "Poaching? We thought *you* were poaching!"

"And I can see why you'd think that," Dan admitted. "Ammon told me how you'd seen me near his mussel farm and out near the craypots." He looked slightly uncomfortable. "I was so busy trying to catch the real poachers in the act that I didn't realize I was being watched."

"It's just that you said you weren't interested in fishing," Toni interrupted. "And then you were on a big fancy fishing boat and going diving near the pots and everything . . ." Her voice trailed off, and she twisted her hair in her hands. "It didn't add up."

"And Uncle Ammon acted like he didn't know you when you came the first day, then he went out with you at night," Wiremu added, wagging a finger suspiciously. "Why did you do that?"

"Well, for starters, I didn't expect Toni to be sitting behind a pile of crates in the dark on the wharf late at night spying on me." Uncle Ammon grinned and Toni squirmed. "And I didn't feel like I was sneaking. Dan and I just had to go out at night because that was when we suspected we'd catch these poachers in the act. They've been diving near the pots at night so they wouldn't be seen during the day."

Jerry finally spoke. "But how come you acted like you didn't know the boat when Dan came here the first day?"

His father shook his head. "Just a precaution. Dan was undercover, and you never know who might have been watching offshore if I suddenly waved like we were old friends." He held out both hands. "I didn't know you all were already on his case—and I still don't know how."

Toni raised her hand slightly. "Umm . . . actually, it was my fault. I kept seeing him—Dan—and I had thought that he—you . . ." She nodded toward Dan. "I thought you were really nice on the ferry, and you knew so much about the dolphins that it didn't seem like you should be doing anything wrong, and so it didn't fit that you were acting—different." She shrugged. "That's what made me suspicious."

Dan smiled. "Ah, so the key is not to be nice in the future. I'll remember to tell them that the next time I'm training new officers."

"But also . . ." Toni frowned again. "When I heard you down at the wharf, you said that we were decoys."

"That's right." Wiremu spoke up. "We thought we were supposed to be helping you with the fishing. You mean you didn't really need our help?"

Uncle Ammon held up his hand. "Oh, believe me, I really have appreciated your help. But we also thought that if people saw me occupied with a group of children they might think it would be easier to move in on our pots."

"All two hundred of them." Dan grinned at Wiremu, who blushed slightly. "When you told me you were coming out to help your uncle I figured you were Ammon's nephew, but then when you said two hundred pots I thought I might have to have to a word with him about exceeding his license."

"Two hundred pots?" Uncle Ammon raised one eyebrow. "Sounds like another big fish story to me."

They all laughed, and even Wiremu joined in. Then Taseu pointed at Dan's uniform and said, "Well, I want to know how you get to do your job. It sounds like it'd be fun."

Dan laughed. "Not too much fun. Lots of hard and interesting work, though."

"Looking after fish?" Erana looked doubtful. "I thought they looked after themselves."

They all laughed, especially Dan, and he leaned his elbows back on the step before he answered. "It would be nice if it were that easy . . . Erana, wasn't it?"

She nodded, and Dan smiled and explained. "The fish probably could look after themselves if the humans weren't so selfish. We have to make sure that everybody only catches what they need, and that there's plenty for everybody."

Uncle Ammon joined in. "That's why the fishermen have a license and a certain amount of fish we're allowed to catch for the markets." He rested his foot on the bottom step. "But when poachers start taking fish near our pots, we lose our livelihood. When I suspected that was happening, I let the Ministry know," he said, pointing to Dan. "And Dan came out to do some surveillance."

"So did you catch anybody?" Taseu's eyes widened, and his voice dropped a tone. "Did you catch them in the act?"

"Not exactly." Dan lowered his voice to match Taseu's. "But we did identify the boat they were fishing from, and we saw them give the catch to someone heading back on the ferry. We were able to call ahead, and I just heard that they were picked up when they docked." He leaned forward. "That's what I'd come to report to Ammon about."

"And that's where I had to go this morning while you were swimming," Uncle Ammon explained. "That's when I told Dan all about our resident detectives."

Dan sat back and pulled a small package from his trouser pocket. It was an envelope, and he flipped back the seal and held out a small, round badge.

"I thought that even though you were hunting the wrong guy, you all were still being very observant." He held it up, and Toni could see the orange fish on top of the white background. She leaned closer to read the words that encircled the fish.

"Junior Fisheries Officer," Erana read out loud for them, twisting her head to follow the writing as it circled the badge.

"That's right." Dan counted out five badges and passed one to each of the children. "We like to award these to children who keep an eye on the fishing limits and know the regulations when they go out with their parents. Even though you didn't do exactly that, I think you still showed you were very aware of what was right or wrong."

Uncle Ammon nodded. "I probably didn't handle the situation too well by just keeping quiet, but I was so uptight about catching these poachers that I didn't realize you were all taking it so seriously."

Toni held the badge lightly between her fingers, then she tapped it thoughtfully and said, "I still have another question." She bit on her lip and pointed toward the ocean. "Before we came over here we read about a man's body being found.

Jerry said it wasn't on one of your lines, but . . ."
She took a deep breath. "That night at the wharf,
you said something about a man called Bob, and
that he wouldn't be in the way for long."

"And that you were going to get rid of him,
just like the other guy," Wiremu added. He put his
hands on his hips. "How do you explain that?"

Uncle Ammon looked puzzled at first, then he
stared at Dan and raised one hand to slowly rub
his forehead as a wide grin spread across his face.

Dan smiled too. "You kids really don't miss a
trick, do you?" He stood up and gestured toward the
wharf. "But I can explain that part of the mystery as
well."

They all followed him down to the wooden
jetty where he pointed out to the sleek white boat
anchored out in the channel.

"Watch this." He put his finger and thumb to
his lips and blew a shrill whistle. Within seconds
the children saw a dark fin rise out of the water
and circle around by the boat.

"Meet Bob." Dan folded his arms and waited
for their response.

"Bob's a dolphin?" Taseu screwed up his face.
"Bob's not a man?"

Dan shook his head. "Bob's a dolphin—a personal friend of mine."

"A pet?" Toni looked up hopefully.

"Not a pet." Dan shook his head. "Bob got caught in nets some months ago, and we've been caring for him over on the mainland. I was using this time at the island as an opportunity to get him back into the wild. Unfortunately he's s little bit friendly. He won't go away."

"So that's why he was swimming with you at the pots," Erana chipped in. "We thought he was a shark, but then you started playing with him."

"And that was confusing." Toni put her hand to her cheek. "You looked like you were up to something bad, but you were playing with a dolphin. It didn't make sense." She hesitated. "But if this is Bob, who was the other guy you were talking about at the wharf . . . the one you got rid of before?"

Dan shook his head. "I can't believe how a conversation can be taken so wrongly." He held up two fingers. "There were actually two dolphins caught in the net. Bob and the other one we called Bill. We released Bill some weeks ago."

"So the other 'guy' you got rid of was Bill the dolphin . . . not the dead man?" Wiremu shot an embarrassed look at his uncle. "Man, we really did get everything wrong. We were thinking you two must be murderers or something. We didn't know what to do."

"Except that Jerry wouldn't believe that you'd do anything wrong," Toni added quietly. "He trusted you completely even when we gave him all our evidence."

Uncle Ammon stared out at the water for a time before he reached out and put his good arm around Jerry's shoulders. "Then it's about time I lived up to that trust." He gave a short laugh. "Before the Coffin House Kids get me into any more trouble."

* * *

"Well, I felt really silly when they said that our dolphin man was a fisheries officer." Toni shook her head as she sat down on her tree branch at the Cliff Hanger. "I can't believe I thought that he was a bad guy."

Jerry looked down at the faintly moving water in the bay beneath the old pohutukawa tree. "I think it was reasonable to think what you did. He certainly appeared to be in all the wrong places— or right places, depending how you look at it." He nodded thoughtfully. "I think you were right to suspect him . . . even my dad, although I didn't like to think about that."

Taseu folded his arms and leaned back against the bank. "I just keep thinking I'd like to be a fisheries officer," he said. "Dan said they do all sorts of things to catch the bad guys." He held up his hand to form a gun and made a popping noise with his mouth.

"He said they arrest them; he didn't say they shoot people," Erana corrected him, putting her hand on his as if to put the gun down. "I'm just glad Uncle Ammon wasn't guilty or anything."

"Same," they responded unanimously.

"But to have even thought he might be a murderer." Toni shook her head. "I'm so glad that's cleared up."

"It makes me feel bad about the man who drowned, though." Wiremu stared up at the leaves moving gently above his head. "I was glad when Dan said that he hadn't been a drug guy or murdered or anything, but to think he was alone in the water all that time . . . just drowning."

"And his kids were waiting for him to come back from his fishing trip," Erana said with a shiver. "Hearing about him drowning really makes me want to see my dad again."

They were all silent for a long time thinking about their own families, then Wiremu cleared his throat. "Well, you know what? We may have made a bit of fools of ourselves, but I'm really glad we came to the island. I sort of feel like it's our island." He waved his arm across the bay, just missing Jerry's head.

Jerry exaggerated a ducking motion and frowned at his cousin. Then he said, "I have a confession to make."

"You mean you've been poaching the crayfish?" Wiremu grinned, then he realized that Jerry wasn't smiling. "Oops, are we talking serious?"

"Sort of serious." Jerry half smiled, then he actually looked embarrassed. "It's just that, when I heard you were all coming over, even though some of you were cousins and everything . . . I wasn't sure that I wanted you here."

Toni watched as he kicked the ground with his foot. She thought back to their first day and how quiet he'd been. They had been so excited about their holiday that they hadn't noticed he really hadn't wanted them there.

"I guess we are a bit much all at once," she offered quietly. "But we only wanted to help."

"And you did," Jerry said, looking up quickly. "I soon changed my mind—honest." He bit his lip. "I don't think my dad would have made the effort about drinking or church or anything if you guys hadn't been such a good example."

"You mean we did something right?" Wiremu asked jokingly, but Toni could tell he understood his cousin. He and Jerry looked at each other, and she was again reminded of how physically alike they were.

"I guess you did," Jerry agreed. He stood up and patted the gnarled gray branch he'd been sitting on. "And I guess I'm trying to say that there's a place in the old Cliff Hanger any time you all want to come and visit."

* * *

"That was so awesome." Toni leaned her folded arms on the top of the metal railing and swayed with the motion of the ferry, watching the dark greens and grays of the island gradually blurring into one dark shape against the blue ocean. She felt Rima press against her leg and gave a big sigh. "I wonder when we will go back."

"Uncle Ammon said next Christmas would be a good time, or just after," Wiremu said from beside her. "You know another thing that's been good about this week? I've found another cousin. I mean, I've always known Jerry, but I never really knew him that well." He stared out at the waves. "I think I'm glad Uncle Ammon broke his arm."

Toni giggled. "In a way I am too. Is that bad?"

"I don't think so." Wiremu watched the sea rolling by the side of the boat and tumbling into white, frilled furrows. "If you think about it, things do happen when the Coffin House Kids are around. Uncle Ammon got help with fishing when he needed it. Jerry got his dad back from drinking and everything . . ."

"And back to church," Toni added. "And I got a new mother."

"That's a big one." Wiremu looked sideways. "And I got a new cousin and uncle."

"You and Erana," Toni corrected, then laughed. "And Taseu has a new career planned."

"Hey, can you see the dolphins?" Erana squealed as she and Taseu broke through the doorway behind them at the same time. "There's heaps of them!"

They all leaned over the rail to watch a group of silvery bodies appear at the side of the boat, rising and falling just beyond the wake. Suddenly, a young dolphin leaped high out of the water, and the sunlight reflected off its wet back as it arched through the air and plummeted back down into the water.

Toni's caught her breath at the beauty and grace of the animal, then she thoughtfully rubbed Rima's head. "We're going home, Rima."

ABOUT THE AUTHOR

Pamela Carrington Reid is a native of Auckland, New Zealand, and resides there with her husband, Paul. They are the parents of five children. Pamela graduated from Auckland University with a double major in English and Geography and has had several articles published in the *New Era, Friend,* and *Ensign*.